Graywolf Press

Camellia Street

Mercè Rodoreda

TRANSLATED AND WITH AN INTRODUCTION BY
David H. Rosenthal

FOREWORD BY
Sandra Cisneros

GRAYWOLF PRESS   SAINT PAUL   MINNESOTA

Published by permission of Institut d'Estudis Catalans, Barcelona
Copyright © 1966 Mercè Rodoreda
English translation © 1993 David H. Rosenthal
Foreword © 1993 Sandra Cisneros

Publication of this volume is made possible in part by a grant provided
by the Minnesota State Arts Board through an appropriation by the Minnesota State Legislature, and by a grant from the National Endowment
for the Arts. Additional support has been provided by the Andrew W.
Mellon Foundation, the Lila Wallace-Reader's Digest Fund, the Mc-
Knight Foundation and other generous contributions from foundations,
corporations, and individuals. Graywolf Press is a member agency of
United Arts, Saint Paul. To these organizations and individuals who
make our work possible, we offer heartfelt thanks.

Published by GRAYWOLF PRESS
2402 University Avenue, Suite 203, Saint Paul, Minnesota 55114

ISBN 1-55597-192-x

9 8 7 6 5 4 3 2
First Printing, 1993

Library of Congress Cataloging-in-Publication Data
Rodoreda, Mercè, 1909–
        (Carrer de les Camèlies. English)
        Camellia street : a novel / by Mercè Rodoreda ; translated with an
    introduction by David H. Rosenthal ; foreword by Sandra Cisneros.
            p.   cm.
        I. Title.
PC3941.R57C313   1993
849'.9352 — dc20   93-12588

In memory of M.G.

೨ FOREWORD ೭

by Sandra Cisneros

THERE ARE NO CAMELLIAS ON CAMELLIA STREET. Maybe once, recent or long ago, but not when I was there last spring. "Los calles han sido siempre para mi motivo de inspiración . . ." Rodoreda wrote in a prologue to one of her novels. So it's on the streets of Barcelona I go in search of her.

Of Rodoreda one French critic had said: "One feels that this little working woman in Barcelona has spoken on behalf of all the hope, all the freedom, and all the courage in the world. And that she has just uttered forth one of the books of most universal relevance that love—let us finally say the word—could have written." He was talking of *The Time of the Doves,* a novel introduced to me by a Texas parking-lot attendant—"Don't you know Mercè Rodoreda?" he asked. "García Márquez considers her one of the greatest writers of this century." A recommendation by García Márquez *and* a parking-lot attendant. They couldn't both be wrong. I had the attendant scribble Rodoreda's name on a check deposit slip, and a year later I bought the book and read it cover to cover all in one afternoon. When I was finished, I felt as foolish as Balboa discovering the powerful Pacific.

Who is this writer, this "little working woman" who arrived too many years too late in my life, but just in time. What I know of Rodoreda I've gathered from introductions, prologues, blurbs, book jackets—bits and pieces from here and there that tell me facts, that tell me nothing. I know she was born on the tenth of October (1909 according to one source, 1908 according to another), an only daughter—like me—of overprotective parents, but unlike me, she is an only child. At twenty-five, she publishes her first novel. At thirty, she receives a prestigious literary prize for her book *Aloma.* She is a prolific writer in the years before the Spanish Civil War, writing novels, publishing short stories in several important literary journals. Was she married? Did she have children? Did her husband want her to follow her life of letters, or did he say, "Mercè, enough of that, come to bed already"? And when she went to bed, did she wish he wasn't there so she could go to bed with a book? I don't know for certain, but I wonder.

I know with the war she takes refuge for a time in Paris—and later, Geneva. Some of her books—*The Time of the Doves* for example, are finished in Geneva, where David Rosenthal, her English translator, says she eked out a survivor's existence, but what exactly does he mean? Did she mop bathrooms and tug bed linens taut, type doctoral dissertations, wipe the milk moustache from the mouth of a small child, embroider blue stars on sheets and pillow-cases? Or work all day in a bakery like Colometa, the pro-tagonist of *The Time of the Doves,* her fingers tired from tying ribbons into bows all day? I can't know.

For two decades when she lived exiled from her lan-guage, Rodoreda does not write. At least, she does not publish. I know she has said during this time she couldn't bear the thought of literature, that literature made her feel like vomiting, that she was never as lucid as during this pe-riod when she was starving. I imagine myself the months I lived without English in Sarajevo, or the year I lived with-out Spanish in northern California—both times not writ-ing because I could not brave repeating my life on paper. I slept for hours, hoping the days would roll by, my life dried and hollow like a seed pod. What would a writer do not writing for a year? For twenty?

She is in her early fifties when she begins to write again, her masterpiece—*La Plaça del Diamant*—(*The Time of the Doves*), the story of an ordinary woman who happens to survive the extraordinary years of a war. A few years later Rodoreda finishes *El Carrer de les Camelies* (*Camellia Street*). 1966. Rodoreda is fifty-eight years old.

When I first arrive in Barcelona the spring of 1983, Rodoreda is dying, but I don't know she exists. It will be years till I meet the Texas parking-lot attendant who first pronounces her name for me. I'm wandering the streets of Barcelona without enough money to eat. I spend the day looking for Gaudí buildings, walking instead of riding the bus to save money. When I have seen all the Gaudí I can manage, I buy the train ticket back to the French-Italian border where I live. I have enough pesetas left to buy a roasted chicken. On the train ride back, I devour that bird like a crazy lady.

May of 1992, the spring before the Olympics. It's Sunday. I'm in Barcelona again, this time to promote my books. I'm staying at a hotel on Las Ramblas. This time, I don't have to go without eating. My meals arrive on a shiny tray with linen folded into stiff triangles and bright silverware and a waiter who opens his arm like a magician.

"I want to go here," I say, pointing on the map to La Plaça de la Font Castellana where Camellia Street begins.

"There?" the taxicab driver says. "But there's nothing there."

"It doesn't matter, that's where I want to go."

We drive past shop windows and leafy boulevards, apartment buildings sprouting graceful iron balconies. I'm going to begin my search in Gracia, the neighborhood of Rodoreda's stories, from the heights of Barcelona where Camellia Street begins and walk downhill toward the Plaça del Diamant. When we arrive finally at La Plaça de la Font Castellana, I realize the taxicab driver is right. There's nothing here but a noisy rotary, a swirl of automobiles and chain link fence, the park below under construction.

Is this La Calle de las Camelias? The buildings boxlike and ugly, walls a nubby gray like a dirty wool sweater. On one corner a plaque verifies "Carrer de les Camelies." There aren't many gardens left anymore. Hardly one. Did they destroy them all in the war?

Pinched between two ugly buildings, a small one-family house from the time of before, something like the house of my grandmother in Tepeyac—several potted plants, a stubborn rose bush, but no camellias. I stand outside the gate peering in like someone trying to remember something. I have arrived too late.

When I can't bear the noise of Camellia Street anymore, the stink of cars and buses and trucks, I duck down a side street, zig-zagging my way the several blocks to the Plaça del Diamant.

It's nothing like I'd imagined. Bald as a knuckle, funny looking as the Mexico City zócalo. Tall apartment buildings hold up the little handkerchief of sky. Light—milky as an air shaft. Were there once trees here do you suppose? Air throbbing with children and motorbikes, goofy teenagers hitting and then hugging each other, schoolgirls on the brink of brilliant catastrophes.

In one corner of the plaza, almost unnoticeable, as dark and discolored as the sad bronze-colored buildings, a bronze sculpture of a woman with doves taking flight— Rodoreda, or Colometa perhaps. Somebody has drawn a penis on her lower torso. Whose kid did this? A dog has left three small turds at the pedestal. Two children race round and round the sculpture, giddy and growling like tigers, and I remember the joy of being chased around the statue of some green somebody—Christopher Columbus?—in Grant Park when I was little.

I've brought my camera, but I'm too shy to take a picture. I choose a park bench next to a grandmother singing and rocking a baby in a stroller. When I don't want people to notice that I'm looking at them, I start writing and it makes me invisible.

Querido agridulce amargura de mis amores,

   I've walked from the Carrer de les Camelies looking for Rodoreda. Here I am in the famous Plaça del Diamant filled with kids and motorbikes and teenagers and abuelitas singing in a language I don't understand.

   And now the boy's soccer game has just begun. A fleet of mothers with babies on their wide hips sail past. A girl with long pony limbs and a camera is shouting "Uria!" to Uria who won't turn around to have his picture taken. Somebody's little one in a stroller stares at me like the wise guy he is, until out of view. A tanned mother, plump as a peach, is being a good sport and playing Chinese jumprope with her girls. The soccer ball thuds on my notebook knocking the pen from my hand. The one with a crooked grin and teeth too big for his mouth arrives with my pen and a shy "perdón."

   Everyone little and big is outdoors, exiled or escaped from the cramped apartments of I can't take it anymore. All of Barcelona here at some age or another to hide or think or pull the plastic caterpillar with the striped whirly-gig, to kiss or be kissed where their mothers won't see them. I think of the park near my mother's house in Chicago, how she can't go there, afraid of the drug dealers. I think of the Los Angeles riots of a few weeks ago. How the citizens of Barcelona own their streets. How they wander fearless in their neighborhoods, their plaza, their city.

   I've come looking for Rodoreda, and some part of her is here, and some part isn't. . . .

What is it about Rodoreda that attracts you to her, a Catalan journalist will ask. I fumble about like one of Rodoreda's characters, as clumsy with words as a carpenter threading a needle.

Rodoreda writes about feelings, about characters so numbed or overwhelmed by events they have only their emotions as a language. I think it's because one has no words that one writes, not because one is gifted with language. Perhaps because one recognizes wisely enough the shortcomings of language.

It is this precision at naming the unnameable that attracts me to Rodoreda, this woman, this writer, hardly little, adept at listening to those who do not speak, who are filled with great emotions, albeit mute to name them.

13 de enero, 1993
San Antonio de Bexar, Tejas

♪ TRANSLATOR'S INTRODUCTION ♪

MERCÈ RODOREDA, THE GREATEST CATALAN NOVELIST of our time and quite possibly the best Mediterranean woman author since Sappho, died of cancer in April 1983. Until now, only two of her books have been available in English: *My Christina and Other Stories* and *The Time of the Doves,* which Gabriel García Márquez called "the most beautiful novel published in Spain since the Civil War."

Rodoreda, born in 1908, came of age literarily during the Spanish Republic—a time when Catalonia was autonomous and its citizens were allowed to speak, write, and study their own language. Between 1932 and 1937 she published five novels, plus numerous shorter pieces in periodicals like *Mirador, La Rambla,* and *Publicitat,* and was recognized as one of the most promising young Catalan authors. With the end of the Civil War in 1939, however, this whole universe collapsed. Catalan books were burned, Catalan newspapers suppressed, and offices were hung with signs saying *No ladres, habla la lengua del imperio es-*

pañol (Don't bark, speak the language of the Spanish empire). Along with half a million other Spaniards, Rodoreda was forced into exile and spent the next few years trying to avoid starvation. She eventually settled in Geneva, where she eked out a grayly anonymous survivor's existence. In an interview with the magazine *Serra d'Or,* she described her state of mind during this period:

> The prewar world seemed unreal to me, and I still haven't reconstructed it. And the time I spent! Everything burned inside, but imperceptibly it was becoming a little anachronistic. And perhaps this is what hurt most. I couldn't have written a novel if they'd beaten it out of me. I was too disconnected from everything, or maybe too terribly bound up with everything, though that might sound like a paradox. In general, literature made me feel like vomiting. I could only stand the greats: Cervantes, Shakespeare, Dostoyevsky. I'm sure I've never been as lucid as I was then, possibly because I hardly ate anything.

Rodoreda remained silent until 1959, when the publication of *Twenty-two Stories* announced her return to the literary scene. After that, she regularly produced novels and became a permanent fixture on Catalan best-seller lists. (*Camellia Street* is now in its fourteenth edition). Since Franco's death, most restrictions on the use of Catalan have been lifted, and in 1979 Rodoreda came home at last, acclaimed as a national spokesperson and adopted as a sort of tutelary saint by a generation of young women writers.

Camellia Street, published in 1966, is the starkest of all Rodoreda's works. It chronicles the life and, obliquely, the times of Cecília C, a street-corner prostitute and later a kept woman in numb, exhausted postwar Barcelona. Cecília, a foundling whose name is written on a scrap of paper pinned to her bib, never takes to her adoptive parents. She flees their stifling attentions and obsessive chatter about her origins as soon as she can—first in search of her father, who has appeared to her in a vision, and then more definitively with her first lover, Eusebi. From this point on her life is, in her own words, spent "searching for lost things and burying dead loves." Incapable of either emotional attachment or shared sensual pleasure, Cecília lives frozen in her own narcissism and anomie. The parallels between her inner life and the disoriented, catatonic Barcelona of the 1940s and 1950s are striking, but Rodoreda never presses the point. Everything is presented from Cecília's point of view, in a stream-of-consciousness similar to that in *The Time of the Doves*. Though not as much of a victim as Jean Rhys's heroines, Cecília resembles them in her helpless, bitter drift through a world of lovers who either quickly bore her or whom she never liked in the first place.

Within her fog of passivity and static self-absorption, however, Cecília longs vaguely but insistently for something else. Sometimes it's another lover, some man whom she can't get for the moment. At other times she craves the emblems of glamour, which she first encounters through her demimondaine "cousins" Raquel and Maria-Cinta. A poor, half-starved streetwalker with all her grand con-

quests ahead of her, Cecília sees a luxurious car and starts
to fantasize:

> I thought someday I'd have a car too and sit in the back
> with a pearl necklace and pearl earrings and a ring with
> a white pearl and a black one and the chauffeur would
> open the door and say "miss" with his cap in his hand.
> And I'd be wearing a pink dress.

More importantly, Cecília craves love from her father, or
from a child. But instead, in her affair with Marc (which
occupies a third of the book), she experiences a perverse
cruelty and jealousy that slowly build into scenes of hallu-
cinatory intensity. The atmosphere of paralyzed claustro-
phobia, petty suspicion and spying, stifled daydreaming
and male brutality that dominates this section is foreshad-
owed by Cecília's first response to her new lover: "I didn't
move and just stared at him like a bird a snake is about to
gobble up." A series of abortions and miscarriages—the
last nearly fatal and provoked by a blow from Marc or one
of his friends—deprives her of any chance to have children. The warmly paternal presence she seeks also eludes
her until the last chapter. Then, after seeking out the night
watchman who had originally found her on a doorstep,
Cecília lets herself become a child again and reaches out
to the old man. Thus *Camellia Street,* a tale of emotional
stupor in a world of moral corruption and self-betrayal,
seems to end on a note of tenuous rebirth:

> I looked around and it seemed like the ceiling was
> higher, the window was bigger and he seemed taller too
> like he'd been growing while we talked and I hadn't no-

ticed. Everything was bigger and I was smaller. I put my feet on the rung under the chair, with my elbows on my knees and my face in my hands. I said very slowly, "I'll buy you a rosebush, a thick wool sweater, a cockatoo and aniseed . . . bushels of aniseed."

To place *Camellia Street* and its author in their proper perspective, the American reader may find some historical background useful. Catalan is a language spoken by approximately seven million people, some of whom live in the Balearic Islands, others in a small strip of southern France that includes Perpinyà (Perpignan), and others in Spain proper, from Alacant (Alicante) to the French border and between the Mediterranean Sea and Aragon. A Romance language, Catalan is closer to Provençal and Italian than to Castilian (the language normally called "Spanish").

The most interesting Catalan literature is of two periods: from the late Middle Ages through the early Renaissance, and from around 1870 to the present. The first era produced such outstanding writers as the lyric poet Ausiàs March (ca. 1397-1459) and the novelist Joanot Martorell (ca. 1410-1468), whose masterpiece *Tirant lo Blanc* was described by Cervantes as "the best book of its kind in the world." During the past century, Catalonia has produced an astonishing body of artistic work. In the visual arts, the genius of figures like Salvador Dalí, Antoni Gaudí, Juli Gonzàlez, Arístides Maillol, Joan Miró and Antoni Tàpies is universally recognized. Catalan writing is of equally high quality, but the world has been slower to become aware of its virtues—partly due to a lack of good translations, and partly because of the Franco government's deliberate suppression.

Since Franco's death, Catalans have moved steadily toward self-government. They now have a bilingual government and a Statute of Autonomy. Free elections to the Catalan parliament recently took place. The study of Catalan is obligatory in the schools, and Catalan daily newspapers, television channels, and radio stations are free to operate. Thanks to authors such as Rodoreda and the poets J.V. Foix, Salvador Espriu, and Vicent Andrés Estellés, Catalan literature has remained as vital as ever. One hopes that these writers, who have spoken so eloquently for and to their nation, will now begin to receive the recognition they deserve in the United States.

David H. Rosenthal

Camellia Street

I have walked many years in this city.—T.S. Eliot

꩜ **I** THEY ABANDONED ME ON CAMELLIA STREET, IN front of a garden gate, and the night watchman found me early the next morning. The people in the house wanted me, but he says at first they didn't know what to do: whether to keep me or give me to the nuns. It was my laugh that won them over, and since they were old and childless they took me in. One lady who lived nearby said maybe my father was a murderer and adopting an unknown child was a big responsibility. The gentleman of the house let the ladies talk. He picked me up, dirty as I was and with a sheet of paper still pinned to my bib, and took me over to look at the flowers: "Look at the carnations," they say he said, "look at the roses, look, look." Because it was spring and everything was in bloom.

But the biggest thing was how the dirtless cactus flowered that night. There was a crumbling wall between our garden and the next one with peeling plaster, and before the plaster fell off it bulged because wood lice burrowed under it, and at the foot of that wall covered with rose bushes, the best of them with white roses, there was a giant cactus. One snowy winter the ground froze and the bottom half of the cactus died, but the top half lived because it had gradually taken root in a crack in that wall with the rosebushes and wood lice. The root lived on bricks and old mortar and fed the cactus, which kept growing till it was higher than the wall and could peek into the next-door garden. And the evening after they found me, a flower bloomed at the top of it with rust-colored outer petals and milky white ones inside and wild disheveled hair at the center. They saw it because there was a moon and they'd left the dining room window open. There were three windows, and they all looked out on a sunken garden you had to climb down a few steps from the kitchen to get to. The moon and the dining room light shone on that flower, and the gentleman, who was having supper, suddenly said "What's that I see out there?" He pointed outside with his fork and the lady went over to the window and said it was a flower and she didn't know how they'd missed seeing the bud. The first time, while I was sleeping. They picked up a candle, went down to the garden, propped a ladder against the wall and I guess they just about drowned in its beauty. When they were about to go to bed the gentleman, whose name was Jaume, said God must have rewarded them by making that cactus, which lived on wall and mortar, burst into flower. And the nicest part is that the flower only came out one night a year on the day they'd found me. Every year the neighbors came to watch, and they had to hurry because it didn't last long.

Before sitting down to supper and noticing the flower,

they'd spent the day talking about me and showing me to the neighbors who came to see me. Some said there was nothing unusual about foundlings, though they'd never seen one themselves, but they'd always heard that people left them on church steps instead of by garden gates. Others said there was a regular time to leave them so the nuns who took them in wouldn't see their mothers. They all got scared when the watchman said he'd spotted me because a black dog was sniffing around. They stripped off my clothes and searched me for bite marks and examined me all over because there was a stain on the ground where they'd found me. One neighbor, Mrs. Rius, said it must be blood and maybe my mother had been bleeding when she left me, but the lady of the house, whose name was Magdalena, said no because if she'd been bleeding there'd be a trail of blood up or down the street and there was only that one spot. They said the strangest thing was the way I laughed when they picked me up and a laughing baby couldn't have bad parents, so I must be a case of love or poverty, a youthful sin, and one lady who died soon afterward grabbed one of my feet and kissed it and said "Poor little thing."

Then they started trying to guess how old I was. One neighbor's husband said they couldn't keep me, that they'd have to report it to the police. They shut him up by saying they'd get around to that later, that first they had to figure out my age. Some said maybe four months, others only two, and one man said he thought it was five. Finally they settled on maybe three. Then they took off the piece of paper stuck to my bib with a safety pin. It had been carelessly torn and the name "Cecília C" was penciled on it. They said it was the handwriting of someone who didn't have much practice, but the gentleman, who never missed anything, pointed out that the "Cecília" was clearer than the "C." Which meant that whoever had written my name couldn't finish it because she was crying and her hand shook when she tried to write. And out of respect for my parents they registered my name just like they'd found it: Cecília C.

⊰ I I SOMETIMES MRS. RIUS WOULD DROP IN AFTER supper. If I was in bed she'd tiptoe into my room and make the sign of the cross over my whole body to protect me. I almost always heard her but I pretended to be asleep, and when she occasionally forgot and didn't come in I wouldn't feel sleepy. The other ladies scared me a little. In the evenings, sitting on the top step that led down to the garden if it was nice out or behind the kitchen door if it was cold, I'd listen to them talking. Their voices came through the window or sounded muffled behind the thick wood. They often talked about my parents. One day they said my mother was probably one of those music hall singers, the kind who dance and have all the men they want and then find they've got a kid without knowing whose it is. Another day they said it must have been a marquise who'd gone to have me across the border saying she was going to a spa and then given me to some poor woman to bring up. The marquise had died and the penniless nurse had gotten rid of me as best she could. One day Senyora Magdalena told them that in April of the year they'd found me, a woman dressed in black with a shiny hairpin had stopped and looked in their garden a few times during the afternoon. She hadn't paid any attention but now it seemed strange. She said the woman was holding a baby who must have been me, and that she was probably looking for a doorstep to leave me on and had chosen theirs because even though it wasn't the doorstep to a mansion you could see they were well-off and had more heart than the owners of a big house—you could tell because there were so many flowers and so well tended. Mrs. Rius always said the same thing: that they shouldn't have registered me with the name on the paper, because if my parents were still alive they'd show up some day and want me back. Everyone disagreed and said no one ever tried to get abandoned children back because even after you've raised them they're more trouble than fun. And even when they're grown they can never repay all the worry they cause. One day Mrs. Rius came by with two old sheets she said I could use. And from then on they made me sleep on hand-me-down sheets.

I grew up sitting on that step and listening to the ladies. I didn't like any of them, and I watched the seeds on the maple tree falling and spinning around like propellers and looked at the sun on the roses. All of a sudden I heard Senyor Jaume say "I'm going up to the tower." As soon as he was gone, they started talking about my father. Senyor Jaume always said he must have been a musician and

that's why he'd named me Cecília. They said he must have
been a wicked man and I had ears like a murderer, with the
lobes flat against my cheeks. My mother must have given
me any old name and Cecília had come out because it was
a sad name. I thought of the seeds spinning around and
around till they lay flat on the ground like me. And my ears
started bothering me. I touched them. They said my father
must be one of those men who try to assassinate the queen
and leave bombs where they know her train will pass and
rob banks, men who only care about burning everything
down. They all imagined him walking for hours and hours
down a road with dust up to his ankles, handcuffed between two civil guards. Because he was so dangerous.
They said maybe he was young, and when they got tired of
saying he was bad they said maybe he was an old lecher
with a mistress and loads of money.

Some afternoons a little old lady with cheeks like wrinkled silk and eyes like blue china would come. She always
acted scared and only visited us once in a while because
she lived far away. According to her, my father must have
been a poor student and my mother a poor girl who became a servant when she was fourteen. Sometimes they'd
make her show them a scar she kept hidden under high
tulle collars reinforced with whalebone. She'd been a
pretty girl and her lover had made her eat barefoot and
when it was time for dessert he made her put her feet on
the table and covered them with kisses. He ended up slit-
ting her throat, but she'd managed to drag herself over to
the window and scream for help, leaving a trail of blood

behind her. One day Mrs. Rius asked if her lover's earlobes had lain flat against his cheeks and she said yes. I was sitting with them and I looked at Senyora Magdalena's elbows, which made me sick because they were always reddish, and while I was looking at them Mrs. Rius slapped my hand and told me not to touch my ears anymore. I still remember the day the color purple came into my life, one summer afternoon with all the blinds drawn so the light only filtered through the cracks. A tall lady walked in wearing a purple dress and a veil with a velvet spot under one eye and a bouquet of violets on her breast and violet shoes, and stroking the violets she said my father must have been a remarkable man because I looked like a nymph or a saint and it was frightening to think how much trouble I'd have with men when I grew up.

Senyor Jaume and Senyora Magdalena wanted me to call them godfather and godmother but I never did. They had two lady cousins who were identical twins, and even though they were a little over thirty they were both *femmes fatales* and had pretty elbows. One was named Maria-Cinta and the other Raquel. Maria-Cinta had a very rich lover and a car, a black one with dark red upholstery, and whenever the car was parked outside the neighbors spied on the chauffeur as he paced to and fro waiting for her. She always went to the Liceu opera house. Raquel's lover had less money. I had a hard time telling them apart but finally I managed it because one dressed more flashily than the other. And from their jewels. Maria-Cinta wore only diamonds. Raquel wore a pearl necklace with a big pearl dangling from the middle. Maria-Cinta sometimes took my face between her hands and said I reminded her of someone she knew, but she never said who. . . . One day she took one of my hands and looked at the top of it and said she hadn't noticed before but she'd never seen a child with such pretty hands; that I must be a pianist's daughter. And I burst into tears.

ꙥ **III**   I WALKED VERY SLOWLY BUT THE GRAVEL STILL crunched and the gate creaked when I opened it. The ladies were talking in the kitchen. I thought that creak would warn them and the next thing I knew they'd grab me and lock me in my room so I couldn't run away again and I'd die locked up, pounding on the door and kicking it. And once I was dead and buried, I'd never be able to look for my father. I went out looking for him because the night before while I was drifting off to sleep, I saw a shower of stars in all the colors of the rainbow falling from the ceiling, and among them I saw his face, looking very blurred.

The sun beat down on the garden and the leaves were drooping. As I passed the tobacco shop, the lady who ran it came out to sprinkle the street and asked where I was going. I broke into a run without answering her and didn't know if my heart was pounding because she'd seen me or because it was the first time I'd gone out alone. I walked down the sunny side of the street and my shadow followed me, reaching halfway up the wall. After walking a long time, since my temples were throbbing like a big clock, I stopped in front of a garden full of flowering hydrangeas.

At the entrance to the house, beside three marble steps streaked with black, there was a pole with a bar across it and on that bar a white bird with a pink crest, his beak turned inward toward his neck and one claw tied to a brass chain. He didn't move, and I felt like he was staring at me. I was rooted to the spot. All of a sudden he jumped, gave a squawk, and ruffled the feathers on his head. The spell was broken by a girl who asked me what the bird's name was; she was blond, with curls, holding a gentleman's hand. I thought right away he must be her father. They'd stopped to watch the bird, who slowly turned around so his back was to us. The gentleman was standing between me and the girl. He was tall and thin, had a strong mimosa smell, and there were dark blue stones on his cufflinks that glittered from time to time. I took his hand without looking at him and had to shut my eyes because I felt like everything was spinning around. When I opened them again, I saw the girl with the curls standing next to me, glaring. Without saying a word, she gave me a rap where my hand was holding her father's and then tugged at his to get him away. They went down the street, and I couldn't understand why instead of leaving with the girl that gentleman hadn't let her go on looking at the bird and come with me. I followed them for a while. Every now and then the girl took a leap and her curls fluttered and when she jumped her father pulled her arm to make her go higher. I got tired of following them, and they grew smaller and smaller. The girl with the curls had a pleated skirt and skinny legs.

I had some trouble finding my way home. As soon as I

got there, I ran to look at my hair. In the living room, above a little table beneath the window, there was a heart-shaped mirror. The frame was made of pink glass flowers with green glass leaves. I picked up one corner of the curtain and draped it over the back of an armchair so more light would come in. My hair was chestnut colored and glossy. I jumped to make it flutter but then I couldn't see my face in the mirror. I could feel it falling against my neck, straight and sad. Sad like me. Because I felt sad about lots of things. I fixed the curtain, sat down in the armchair and stayed there a long time looking at my hands.

When it started getting dark, I went up to the tower. I'd never been there before and I remember that first time because I was still scared the tobacco shop lady had told on me for running away. Senyor Jaume took me. We started up the stairs to the roof, and before we got there he told me to hold onto his pants so I wouldn't fall. It was dark at the top of the stairs and he said how years before he'd meant to put in a lightbulb. He took off an iron bolt, lifted a latch, and stepped down to open the door, which swung open on the inside, and we stepped out onto the roof.

To get to the tower, we had to climb some wooden steps with no railing that started in the storeroom. The tower had windows on all four sides. There was a flagpole outside the one looking out on Camellia Street. There were pictures on the few patches of wall between all those windows: a flying lady with a blue silk sash, a bearded man with snakes around him, a big open hand covered with wrinkles, and a man with no skin, seen from the front and back. Senyor Jaume showed them to me one by one and said I wouldn't go to school because he'd teach me everything a little girl should know, and more. He sat down in a yellow easy chair he'd dragged over so it was in front of that cut-off hand and with a bamboo pole he'd pulled up from some soft dirt in the back garden, he showed me a mountain on the hand and asked if I knew what it was called. He asked me three times, and the last time he told me and then repeated it three times because that way he said the names I learned would be engraved in my memory. He said every evening, while the women chatted downstairs, he gazed at the sky. And he turned his chair till he'd gone all around so he could look out each window awhile. The west one last of all.

IV LIKE THE BLUE SCARF SENYOR JAUME PUT ON AT the first sign of cold weather and didn't take off till spring, I had a scarf around my neck that nearly choked me. The doctor pushed my tongue down with a spoon handle and looked at my tonsils. The medicine burnt going down and made me groggy, and before I dozed off Senyora Magdalena gave me lime-flower tea to make me sweat. Everything was hot and everything tasted awful and their voices came muffled through rows and rows of wet curtains. Their faces were blurry like my father's when I saw it that time among those stars. Sometimes I saw just their eyes and sometimes just their mouths. At night my fever got worse and that scarf was smothering me but when I tried to pull it off I couldn't grab onto anything: like I was fighting a cloud of smoke. When I did get up, I felt like they'd given me a new pair of legs. They couldn't walk or run or clatter; they were like springs, stretching and scrunching up while I wobbled on top of them.

All because I'd run away and gone to the opera. Senyora Magdalena'd pulled an armchair up to the window and put a pillow behind my head with a lacy, ribbony pillowcase. I sat there for hours and hours, watching the cactus turn ashy gray, stabbed from inside by yellow thorns. Senyora Magdalena set my lunch down on a little table and without looking at me, or sometimes looking like she wanted to learn me by heart, said I was lucky to have fallen into such good hands because in other houses they'd have made me pay for running away with black and blue marks all over my body. But she didn't tell the neighbors about the opera. She said I was sick because her husband made me study too much and learn things too hard for someone my age, but it'd be worse in a school with nuns because the girls would catch on right away that no one knew where I came from. And they'd treat me like dogs with puppies who won't nurse a kitten even if you slip it under their bellies. And then they'd bully me till I left the school.

And I was sick because I'd worried so much about running away. Scared to death of doing something naughty but dying to go ahead and do it; my terror, when it was time to go home, that I wouldn't be able to find the house. Ever since that afternoon when I'd gone out looking for my father, and I never knew if they'd noticed, they kept the front

gate locked. They said there were thieves in the neighborhood, that they had to live behind closed doors. I stared at
those iron bars that kept me in, and one day I thought I'd
jump the wall and get away down the street. Sometimes I'd
pull thorns off the bougainvilleas and rosebushes along
one side of the bars, so I wouldn't get too scratched when I
climbed up to jump over. The bars ended in some thin
spikes, but I only climbed halfway up, to a frieze made of
circles. When I'd caught my breath, I clutched a branch
from an olive tree in the next yard and, with a great effort,
pulled myself along it till I could sit on our neighbors' wall,
which was pretty thick. Slowly, holding on tight to the
edge, I let myself down that wall. By the time my feet
touched the ground, my knees were skinned and my arms
were trembling. I was nervous. When I was pretty far away,
I asked an old lady who was sitting on the sidewalk knitting how I could get to the Liceu opera house, and she said
you just keep going toward the sea. I got to a big prome-
nade lined with trees. I stopped, thinking I was lost. Right
away I caught the smell coming from the branches. Cool.
And when I thought about it that cool smell mixed with
the hot one from my medicine when I was sick. It was dark
out and there were lights and noises all around. I kept
walking for a long time. The days when I had the worst
fever, I imagined the blue shirt fronts and gray feathers on
the guards at the entrance, the beaks on those gold birds
that were lights, the red velvet and that old hunched-over
man surrounded by fancy lords wearing hose, singing and
singing away. And the golden birds, the feathers, the blue

shirt fronts and red velvet all mixed with the fever, dissolving like things you see just before you fall asleep till among wisps of fog a diamond cross that looked like it was made of fire and water came closer and closer.

I just wanted to watch the musicians go in and see what they looked like, but the crowd swept me along: ladies in tulle, with silk dresses, gentlemen with white flowers in their lapels and a shiny ribbon down each side of their pants. A boy who opened carriage doors looked at me awhile and then asked what I was doing there. He was raggedy, with a spit curl on his forehead. I told him I wanted to see the musicians, and he said I couldn't see them, that they'd gone in another door. And he laughed like he was very happy and when the fever was devouring me I'd see that lock of hair and his two rows of white teeth. The crowd pushed us apart and carried me toward the door. While that tea was scalding my tongue, I saw shoes with diamonds and coats with long furs, as if the prettiest animals had come to hear the singing, and that tight dress covered with strings of jangling pink beads. I reached out to touch them but they slipped through my fingers. And everything I saw hurt. They said I was very sick and could hardly breathe because the chill had gotten deep inside me. It must have been when I stopped under the orange awning outside that big café. I just looked at the people, because I didn't know which way to go. They'd thrown me out by the scruff of the neck like a cat, and they wouldn't have seen me if I'd stayed sitting down but I went down the aisle to see the musicians, who were playing below the stage. And as they took me outside, one of those men with blue shirts and feathers on their hats started laughing because he thought I was so funny.

The terrace outside that café was full of ladies who looked like Maria-Cinta: dressed in black, with low necklines, their legs crossed and that bit of white frilly lace at the bottoms of their skirts. Some wore little crosses or pretty jewels between their breasts. It was Maria-Cinta who spotted me, and afterward she always said she'd thought she was seeing things. She shot up like someone had stuck her with a pin and asked what I was doing there. I couldn't answer because I was looking at that diamond cross I'd never seen before. And Maria-Cinta and her friend, who was tall and graying at the temples, took me home in the car our neighbors always gaped at, when I thought I'd end up in the sea because a man had told me if I went too far I'd fall in. And that the sea likes little girls. And Maria-Cinta's gentleman friend, who smelled of tobacco smoke and cologne, took me on his lap, and while the car rolled along and the lights from the streetlamps flickered in and out, I stuck my hand between his jacket and his vest, way up under his arm, and left it there. And the hand and I both felt good.

V THE FIRST EVENING I WENT BACK UP TO THE tower I saw a huge star above the mountains. Senyor Jaume came up close, looked where I was looking, and said that was the brightest star, mine. And he told me to wave to it. . . . In those days, when it was hot out we read in the garden and when it got cooler we watered the plants. My legs were almost as strong as before and I could run and jump. I'd learned lots of things. I knew the names of all the little bones in my hands and feet, and before falling asleep I liked to say them over to myself. I could add, subtract and multiply but not divide. I knew the names of oceans and rivers. The names of lots of flowers. But I never could remember what air was made of. Or water. We watered the plants at dusk so the sun wouldn't make the dirt bubble and kill them. It seemed like it would hang there forever, bewitched at the tips of the top leaves on the mock orange bush, which only saw it as it set. I watered around the borders, the little plants. He did the big ones and the camellias, so delicate, because only he knew how to sprinkle them without disturbing the dirt. The camellias lived on one side of the fence. On the other side were the bougainvilleas. He kept them in little casks of earth fertilized by chestnut leaves, and the casks were buried and covered with a thin layer of dirt. Red camellias and white camellias, pink-and-white-speck-led camellias, stemless, lying flat against the branches like they were dead. We watered the lilies last, in their flower bed in the middle.

One day when I was sitting with my nose in a book I felt someone watching me through the fence. All I could see was a shadow flitting to and fro, but I kept on reading and pretended not to notice. That night I thought I should have looked to see who it was. A few days later the same thing happened again, but first I heard a whistle. I looked up and saw a boy. The sun was in my eyes, so I couldn't see him very well. He was in rags, with a spit curl in the middle of his forehead. We stared at each other for a while without saying a word and finally, when I recognized him, I went over to the bars and asked how he'd found out where I lived. He said that night at the Liceu he'd followed me when they threw me out because he'd seen how little I was and was worried and how when that gentleman and lady had taken me away in their car he'd climbed on the back. He said he'd come lots of times because he liked to look at little gardens around houses, and that he lived in a shack with his brother. All of a sudden they called me from inside and he took off like a shot.

I still remember how that afternoon, when the sun was setting, instead of watering Senyor Jaume had me put on a clean dress and we went to buy plants at a nursery. We stopped to look in the window: there were roses with one side of their petals dark orange and the other yellow like broom. Roses dark on the inside and light on the outside. Dwarfs, nothing but buds waiting to open, and rose moss with flowers somewhere between pink and lavender. There was a red one, all by itself and one of the reddest, with a few drops on its petals, as if it had been crying. There was no one around when we entered, and the gardener took his time coming out. His hands were covered with dirt, big and with knobbly fingers, but when he picked up a flower he acted like he was afraid of bruising it, as if he'd made it himself without knowing how but he was sure if he grabbed it roughly it would fall apart, so he held it gently, after wiping his hands on his pant legs. He blew on it to separate the petals, and when it was open, he held it between his fingertips so we could see the petals' color when they're born. Senyor Jaume said he'd never been able to get tuberoses to grow in his garden, how maybe the air wasn't right and that's why they weren't happy there. Then the gardener put the flower with that funny color in a vase with some others and said "Follow me." We walked through the store and across a little court-yard, climbed a few steps and went out into a field of flow-ers. There were seedbeds, little plants just sprouting in neat rows along strings, and we walked to the middle of the field, which was divided by a thick viburnum hedge, and before we got to the other side, a wave of fragrance hit us from a big patch of tuberoses. Senyor Jaume took off his hat, his hand fell against his thigh like his hat and hand were both made of lead, and he whispered "My God. . . ."

He bought a rosebush pruned so it was round like a ball with lots of little open roses. He leaned it against his shoulder and told me kick aside any stones I saw so he wouldn't stumble, since he couldn't see a thing. We planted the bush as soon as we got home, at the bottom of the steps leading to the kitchen. The roses were pink, in clumps, but the pink was whitish in the oldest ones. They were born pink but died white. And every branch was like a bouquet, with lots of open ones and lots of closed ones. To make sure he'd planted it right, Senyor Jaume got down on his knees, checked that it was straight, and sent me to fetch a bottle of ink. He had me hold it while with the edge of a leaf he'd dipped in it he blacked out the name of the rosebush written on a little piece of yellow wood tied to the trunk with a wire and started writing on the side of the wood where there'd been nothing written. He made me read it and it said: Cecília.

Lots of nights, when it was nice out, I'd wait for the sun to come up in that garden. Because of my rosebush.

VI SHE WAS A SHORT NUN, WITH YELLOW SKIN ON her face and a nose like a hazelnut. She spoke with her hands up her sleeves but I saw them because she took them out to dab a runny eye with a very white, neatly pressed handkerchief. The skin on her hands, with their clean, carefully trimmed nails, was the same color as the skin on her face. She said sure, they'd make the dress because they took in lots of girls and what they wanted was work so the girls could keep busy. But she said they shouldn't expect it quickly because they were loaded down with other jobs.

It seems I was so sick that they'd thought I was going to die, and one night when they thought I had died because they couldn't find my pulse and I was breathing softer than a mouse, they both promised the Virgin Mary that if she saved me they'd give her a silk dress embroidered with gold and jewels. As soon as I was out of danger, they started saving money and when they thought they had enough they began looking for a convent that would make the dress, but none of them wanted to do gold embroidery because they said they didn't know how, that they just did monograms on sheets and pillowcases with cotton thread, and when they finally found some nuns who could do gold embroidery, the price they quoted was so high that they didn't get the order. But that short nun agreed right off the bat and said she'd go and measure the Virgin, or maybe it would be better if the priest lent them an old dress, because that way they'd have a clearer idea of the neck and arm measurements, how much silk they'd need and everything else. A few days after they got the old dress, they sent us an estimate, and it was reasonable.

They made a dress and cape with thick silk and gold stitching at the bottom of the skirt and around the cape. In the middle of the skirt, in front, there were curlicues and flowers with gold thread and in the middle, above the flowers, there was a chalice, and above the chalice, like a crown, five flowers Senyora Magdalena thought were roses with a jewel in the middle of each one, and all the jewels were different colors. When we went to get the dress, the nuns opened the box and lifted a piece of tissue paper on top. Everything shone so bright it was scary, and my hands started shaking and I whispered "A yellow stone." And Senyor Jaume, beside me, said "A topaz." And me, "A blue stone." And him, "A turquoise"; a red one, a ruby; a clear one, a diamond. . . . And the nuns stood there chuckling.

All our neighbors came to see the dress. We laid it out flat on a table and Mrs. Rius grumbled because she would have liked all the jewels on the flowers to be the same

color and she said those nuns must be a little nutty. But
everyone else said they'd done a fine job and defended the
dress from top to bottom. We took it to the church and
they thought the priest would welcome them but it was
only the sacristan, who thanked them for the Virgin and
the priest. Every Sunday we went to Mass to see if they'd
put the dress on the Virgin. And she was always wearing a
different one. But one afternoon I climbed over the wall in
my red dress because I'd set fire to some newspapers and I
went into the church and looked up at the altar and it
seemed like the Virgin was wearing our dress. I climbed
the steps. The church was empty and calm, with a sea of
flickering candles: some straight and some leaning. I
touched the dress and ran my fingers along the embroidered flowers and touched the stones. I went out and ran
through the streets and when I got home they had to open
the gate for me and I was so out of breath I could hardly
get the words out to tell them the Virgin was wearing that
dress. We all went to see her and Senyor Jaume whispered
that the Virgin might have finer gowns but none so elegant, with those jewels that seemed to sparkle with laughter because you could see those nuns were the jolly kind.

We went to make the final payment. They had to pay for
the dress in three installments because the money they'd
saved wasn't enough, and a young nun with rosy cheeks
and a lily-white forehead opened the door, and when she'd
gone Senyora Magdalena told me she was a novice, that
she still had her hair and wasn't wearing a ring but when
she married Our Lord they'd cut her hair and put a ring on

to separate her from everything. That she'd dress in white for her wedding and be all alone among multitudes, because once you've married Christ you're all alone.

When the short nun the novice had gone to fetch came in, she shook my hand so we'd be friends and told Senyora Magdalena she had a very cute little daughter. Senyora Magdalena said I wasn't her daughter, that they'd found me in front of their gate and taken me in, but they loved me like I was theirs and that's why they'd promised to have the dress made when I was dying on account of something silly I'd done. She said I was a good girl but I did some strange things and the nun asked what they were and she told her everything: how I played with fire, lit pieces of paper in the stove from hot coals and then carried them all over the house; how I made paper cones out of stationery and stuck one inside the other and burned them, and sometimes I'd set fire to newspapers. How one day when she had visitors she'd gone in the kitchen to get the sugar bowl and found me in a corner, still as a corpse, with a little burning paper cone stuck in each ear. How when she'd scolded me my lips had turned purple and I'd said I wanted to burn my ears so I wouldn't have any. How to break my bad habit, since they knew I didn't like the color red, she'd made me a red dress and forced me to hem the seams, and the first day I put it on I ran upstairs and locked myself in the tower, where I paced around like I was crazy, from side to side. Every time I couldn't keep from setting fires she'd make me put on that dress and while I was wearing it they called me the flame. I was dying of embarrassment and stared at her wrinkled elbows, because old people's elbows made me sick and I wanted her to turn my stomach. The nun stroked my hair and stood there for a moment without saying anything, just looking. Then she asked if the priest had liked the dress, and Senyora Magdalena said he'd loved it, that he'd come up to them with his arm out and his mouth wide open from laughing so merrily, saying God would repay them even though the Virgin had already performed a miracle by saving Cecília, and to tell the nuns who'd embroidered it they were the best workers in the world, with a golden touch to do gold embroidery. And it was all lies because they hadn't even seen that priest. Then Senyora Magdalena said when I was only three they'd dressed me up as a nun and hadn't been able to get me to change clothes all winter, because if they tried to I'd cry and cry and say my bones were freezing. The nun gave me a picture she fished out of a deep pocket and it was Jesus Christ with the Sacred Heart holding one hand up in blessing. She asked why they'd called me Cecília and they said because it was written on a piece of paper stuck to my bib with a safety pin. The novice with rosy cheeks came back and when the other one saw her she told me not to make any more paper cones out of stationery and asked them to excuse her. And I couldn't figure out why they called the Mother of God "the Virgin" when everybody else called her the Mother of God.

◁ VII Once a week, every Friday, Maria-Cinta sent someone to pick me up and I spent the rest of the day at her place because they said I should see a bit of the world. By eleven o'clock I was ready and when the car stopped in front of our gate, the chauffeur, whose name was Silvestre, blew the horn three times. The first day he asked if I wanted to sit next to him or in back. I said in back and as I was getting in, the wind blew an acacia flower in with me. I lay down on the seat like it was my bed, because I didn't care about watching streets and stuff and what I really wanted, lying there with my eyes shut, was for everything to be like that night at the opera, seeing that hunched-over man pacing back and forth and hearing a woman sitting in front of me with a bracelet shaped like a golden snake telling the man beside her about all the mysteries in that theater: how the ceiling was open and the lights kept you from seeing it and big machines lifted the sloped floor and made it flat for carnival dances. And all the way I kept my hand between the seat and its back and imagined I was smelling tobacco smoke.

By the time I got there my dress was wrinkled. Maria-Cinta had it made out of white etamine, with the hem embroidered with bunches of cherries and another bunch in front—right over my heart, she said.

Maria-Cinta was wearing a Japanese silk dressing gown with flowering almond branches embroidered all over the back. She lived on the Passeig de Gràcia, and from her terrace you could see a mansion with its back garden full of palm trees with fan-shaped leaves and big blue-and-white china pots and, farther away, some more rickety palms on the Diagonal. While she was ironing my dress, Maria-Cinta told me to take a bath. She had a white tub with a yellow band around it. The bar of soap was too big for me to hold and the bottle of cologne was at least a quart. She called the chambermaid to scrub my back and told her I'd run away from home to hear the singing and how the opera I'd gone to see was one she'd seen at least fifty times herself but she couldn't help crying every time the old man with the bells set off with his dead daughter in a sack.

The maid washed my back with a yellow sponge full of holes, much softer than the esparto glove Senyora Magdalena scrubbed me with in the sink. If she was too busy, Senyor Jaume would do it. He put on a dark blue apron with three white stripes at the bottom so he wouldn't splash his pants, and I'd slip my clothes off because Senyora Magdalena'd already unbuttoned them in back. Then he'd grab my arm and say "Forward march!" He'd soap the glove and scrub my back hard, but he made me do the front because he was afraid of tearing my skin. Then he'd rinse me with a saucepan. But sometimes he'd say he was tired and didn't feel like washing me. One day when I'd fallen in the mud and was horrified at being so dirty, he said God had made man out of mud and when I was dry it would flake off by itself.

Maria-Cinta made me stand in front of her, and while she dried me with a bath towel she'd make me show her both sides of my hands. Clean and pretty. Then she'd sprinkle me with powder and make me run around to shake off the extra. The maid would laugh and so would I, because the wind from running tickled and Maria-Cinta would take that diamond cross out of a red box and put it on me. But the chain was too long so she'd knot it a few times and turn on all the lights. She had me look in a mirror that went up to the ceiling and I saw my whole body, but my eyes kept wandering to that diamond cross, which sparkled green and pink in the mirror, like it was joy's own cross. In the afternoons Raquel would come and we'd drink Chinese tea with jasmine.

On Midsummer Night Maria-Cinta and Raquel brought cakes topped with cherries and pine nuts. Our neighbors put everything they wanted to burn out in the street and the kids helped and a few days earlier we'd gone to all the homes in our neighborhood, asking for wood. They built a bonfire right in front of our gate, because it was in the middle of the block, and by the afternoon Senyora Magdalena was already grumbling. She said the house would get all smoky and nagged Senyor Jaume because he wouldn't ask them to move the fire further down. I remember how that year I went out in the front garden while Senyora Magdalena was cooking supper. The light was gray and the street seemed to be asleep. I heard a whistle. The boy from the Liceu came out from behind a woodpile and stood in front of me, slapping his thigh with a stick. He must have realized I was startled because he burst out laughing like he thought he'd scared me. When I asked him where he'd come from I don't think he answered me. We sat down on the front step, not saying a word, staring at the wood, and finally he said he'd like to set it on fire. And I don't know why but I started telling him how the first time I'd gone out by myself I'd come to a street on a hill and outside a house I'd seen a white bird with a pink crest and a chain around one leg, sitting quietly on a brass bar. I could see he didn't quite believe me, but little by little he got all excited about seeing that bird. I couldn't find the house or the street. Then, as we were walking, he said he knew lots of ways to get to Tibidabo, we could go there, and he visited the cemetery all the time. Once he'd stayed on purpose when they locked up. He'd hidden behind some big wreaths so the watchman wouldn't throw him out. He wanted to see the flames. The sky darkened till it was black with scurrying clouds, and just when he was getting sick of waiting he saw them: blue and lavender, with an orange tongue from time to time. Whenever he went there he'd steal flowers off the wreaths and then throw them away because they stank of wax and death.

When we reached the end of the avenue, we stopped to rest awhile. He said his name was Eusebi. There was a breeze and you could see the leaves' shadows fluttering on the ground. Someone set off a rocket down by Montjuíc. It seemed like it had taken off from the sea and broke into pieces like some devil had smashed a star.

᭡ **VIII** I'D HIDDEN SEVEN MARBLES AND A HAIRPIN between the arm and seat on the yellow easy chair in the tower. One marble was clear with thick white swirls that you couldn't tell where they began or ended. Another one, also clear, had swirls the color of lemon peel. Eusebi'd swiped them from a kid who'd left them on the ground in a little bag while he was fighting with an older girl over one of those tops with strings. He'd given me the pin. I kept the marbles for him. He'd asked what I'd like to have that would be all mine, and I'd said a glittery hairpin. We went into a department store, and in the middle of a bunch of ladies looking at a girl demonstrating how you put on makeup, we went up to a counter. When we were out in the street again, he said "Open your hand," and he gave me a pin with three diamond stars. I never found out when or where he'd stolen it. I had to wear it in secret because the day Senyora Magdalena saw it she tried to take it.

Eusebi and I had been pals ever since that night with the fireworks. We'd spent it together beneath the pines. I woke up before him and it was like I'd slept outdoors all my life. I looked at his face, which was close enough to touch. I moved the shadow of one finger across his slitted eye a few times and the slit, which glistened, didn't get bigger or smaller. I pulled a few locks of his hair that stuck out and then smoothed them down with the others. I was wearing an old blue dress, and when I got up I stood on tiptoe with my hands stretched above my head and thought how I was blue like a flame. Then, with the thumb and first finger on each hand, I touched the dimples on my cheeks because Eusebi had said I had a dimple on each one. The sun had just risen and there were wisps of fog among the grass. I stuck out one hand and, leaning a little to one side, I said

"Things are the way they are," because Maria-Cinta always said that and I wanted to be like her. I knelt in front of Eusebi and, to wake him up, I stuck my finger in his ear and thought how maybe it was near the hammer and anvil. Because I knew more than you'd have thought. He blinked a few times, half-dazed, and we looked at each other again like we'd done the night before when, sick of crowds and watching the ferris wheel, we'd headed for the woods. I really didn't want to, but that's how it happened. I felt ashamed of how we'd looked at each other, standing there spellbound in the moonlight, and that's why I told him I sometimes thought about what the sun and moon did when they were little. How the sun was a rotten ball that spattered the night when it set. And how the moon was gnawed by termites with worms in all the holes, like corpses in burial niches. Gnawed like a hunk of cheese and frantically hot, dying without realizing it like our brains. Killed by heaps of worms that wouldn't leave an inch of white. And when the worms were the bosses, everything would fall and the earth would be covered with a crust of squashed grownups and kids. Thick. And I wouldn't get the words out of my mouth because then we looked at each other again like that and all I could say was when the sun and moon fell the earth would still keep turning. As if everything shining in Eusebi's eyes had softened me and there was nothing firm left inside.

But in the daylight I wouldn't let him suck me into his eyes. I got up and started running down the mountain. He called to me saying wait, we'd go to the cemetery. But I ran

home. I found the gate open and ashes scattered around
the street. Senyora Magdalena was dressed and waiting, so
mad she could hardly breathe. She gave me such a hard
slap that I had a nosebleed all morning. After that they
locked me in a lot, but I could always escape with the
neighbors' olive tree.

IX I CAN HARDLY REMEMBER THE WAR. ALL I KNOW
is I liked seeing the grownups so scared and walking down
the middle of the street when the sirens went off, but what
I liked best was that kind of sob they made when it was
over. And that excitement was mixed with shame about my
blood, about staining the sheets that first night. With the
bombings they started drinking lime-flower tea again, and
the tea smelled like trees and fever. In the kitchen, while
Senyora Magdalena measured out the little bit of sugar
they let her have, trying to make it last, I looked at that tan-
gle of leaves and flowers, touching it so my finger would
smell like night and sickness.

They came and told us the church with the Virgin wearing our dress had been burned, and one afternoon I went
to see it. It was the hottest part of summer. A boy from the
militias was coming down the street with his shirt open
and filthy as a pig. I was twelve years old then, though
everyone said I looked fifteen, and that boy must have
been seventeen or maybe a little younger. I looked away
and pretended not to notice but out of the corner of my
eye I could see him coming closer. When he was next to

me he lifted one whole side of my hair with his out-stretched hand and still walking, let the hair slip through his fingers. My heart skipped a beat but I didn't act scared and as soon as I reached the corner I started to run. The church walls were still standing, the ceiling had caved in and everything was bathed in sunlight. I kicked the stones around. Under some bricks I found a lily made of painted wood and a burnt face that must have belonged to some lady saint. The eyebrows and forehead were missing, but you could see the eyes and the mouth was a little open. I kept her, and when I got home I stuck her in a shoebox and hid it under the tower stairs with a piece of old curtain on top. That night I saw her head for a long time; I felt sick to my stomach and couldn't get to sleep till early morning.

Senyor Jaume spent every morning and afternoon run-ning around Barcelona hunting for food. He said their money was almost gone, everything was expensive, and the only good the war had done was to get those cats out of his garden. The day they bombed the town hall, Senyora Mag-dalena was almost sick. While they were shaking with fear, I kept lifting the right side of my hair, letting it slip through my fingers and seeing the face on that boy who must have gone to war and had eyes like a lost dog. The next day I went to sit on a bench by the Passeig de Gràcia and watched the cars go by with flags. Sometimes I'd think about Eusebi, who'd disappeared when the war started. Raquel had managed to get away to London with her jew-els. Maria-Cinta lived alone in her apartment and always kept the balconies shut. At the end of the first summer I went to see her with Senyor Jaume. When we were already in the street, Senyora Magdalena came running out and took a medallion off my neck with a picture of Saint Cecilia they'd given me for my First Communion. Maria-Cinta sent me out onto the terrace. She was wearing that dressing gown with flowering almond trees and her hair all loose like a black wave. The flowers were glossy, pink on the inside and white at the edges. I looked at the palm trees while they whispered to each other. All of a sudden I heard Senyor Jaume say "Aren't you cold?" I thought that was a funny question because it was hot out and I turned around to look at them and he was running his hand along her arm, back and forth from her elbow to her wrist. To keep from seeing more, I ran inside and went in the bathroom. I looked in the mirror but the room was dark, so I turned on the light. And then, for the first time, I realized I was completely different. My legs were rounded where before they'd been straight; under my dress my breasts, still girlish, had begun to stick out a little but to make a crack between them I had to squeeze them with my arms. I looked in my own eyes and felt like I wasn't alone. Almost without noticing, I leaned closer to my face and the mirror clouded over and the mist hid my face from the middle down. I slowly closed my eyes till they were slits to see what I'd look like dead. And then I don't know exactly what happened. I fell in love with myself. I had that blood, and I listened to it pulsing through my body, sometimes sleepily trickling down my silky thigh. I put my hands on the back of my neck and tossed my hair up in the air. My skin was soft and my elbows were soft and I couldn't describe what I felt: that I wasn't like other people, I was different because all alone, surrounded by towels and the smell of soap, outside the mirror was the loveable one and inside the one who loved her.

᠑ **X** PAULINA WAS SKINNY AS A RAIL, WITH COARSE, dry, straight hair. She wore it short and all day long she walked around with a head that looked like it belonged on a crazy woman. Paulina was Mrs. Rius's maid. Mrs. Rius's house was prettier than ours, with four palm trees shaped like umbrellas in her garden. The wrought iron on her gate was fancier and the pots on top of the two pillars on either side had asparagus plants with agaves in the middle. Mrs. Rius's husband had left her three sons who when they grew up treated her like their fiancée, bringing her flowers and choosing material for the dresses she had made. Paulina was seventeen skinny years old and had a quick temper; for any old reason she'd give you the silent treatment for hours and you never could find out what had made her mad.

When the war had been going on for a while, Senyora Magdalena asked Paulina if she'd like to come and clean on Sundays. She said yes but not to tell Mrs. Rius because she'd fire her if she found out she was pulling the wool over her eyes. Apparently Mrs. Rius wanted Paulina to read lives of saints to her on Sundays and it was very dull; to get out of it, some Sundays she'd say she had to go see her cousins even though she didn't have any. The first day she came to clean she went out all dressed up, smelling like a carnation and her hands red with cold, and when we'd shut the door behind her she said to feel her heart, which was pounding like crazy. Halfway through the afternoon, Mrs. Rius rang the bell. Since we'd spotted her through the blinds, we had time to go in the back garden and into the toolshed, where we sat down on a pile of sacks. Paulina sat there for a long time without talking and finally she said that was it, Mrs. Rius would smell the carnation perfume because she had a nose like a bloodhound. Mrs. Rius didn't leave till they were ready to set the table so we had time to chat about lots of things. She told me she was in love with that boy who used to come and see me sometimes before the war and if he'd been coming to see her she'd have died of joy, that she only knew him from seeing him walking along our street with that spit curl over one eye and, even though she hadn't gotten a good look at him, she was sure he had pretty eyes. "But for pretty eyes," she whispered, "there's nothing like the ones right here." Before, for two straight months she'd been in love with Mrs. Rius's oldest son and since she couldn't sleep she'd spend the night polishing his shoes. The reason she'd chosen the oldest, who owned a printing shop, was because he'd never said a word to her and hardly even glanced her way when she brought him his food, while the others almost killed her with pinches. She'd lost interest now, but even so she'd marry that boy with the whistle like a shot; she said she hadn't seen him for a while and did I know where he was. I said no and she said what a pity. The day she'd liked best was when he went by her house running a stick along the iron bars outside. She thought it was funny how someone's whistle could make her fall in love when she was a terrific whistler herself and knew how to stick two fingers in her mouth so her whistle would carry all the way to the rooftops. But she didn't like her own whistle, which was like the whistle when a fire starts. That boy, on the other hand, whistled like a bird and had a flat stomach. And she'd only marry someone with a flat stomach.

When it started getting dark it also started raining and we sat there for a while without talking, just listening to the rain on the roof. Soon drops started coming in and she said if that pitter-patter kept up for long she'd be sleeping like a log. I told her I was a foundling, and she said "Just like Moses." By the time they came to tell us Mrs. Rius had left, we'd become great friends.

Every day we'd go out and sweep the street. First we'd sprinkle it with sand to pick up the dirt. We always swept it at the same time because I wanted to see Mrs. Rius's youngest son when he came home from school. One day, with a broom in her hand, Paulina started laughing to herself and when she'd gotten tired of laughing, she said, winking at me, that she'd like to spent her wedding night with music in the next room. And how she'd like a garden where she could hang a hammock like at the first house she'd worked in. Her mistress was named Carolina and she'd planted lots of crown vetches. And lots of narcissi because she'd been born on Christmas day. She asked if I ever thought about what kind of husband I'd like. She said she was sure all the girls were like her, boy-crazy, but not just to fool around with them; to sleep with them. She took a chicken foot wrapped in brown paper out of her pocket, pulled the muscles so the toes wiggled, and said she liked that foot because it scared her.

XI I NEVER WOULD HAVE THOUGHT THAT SO MANY years later I'd still remember the afternoon we went to see Senyora Rosalia. When she was very young she'd married a widowed notary who had portraits of his first wife, who was also named Rosalia, all over the house. It was an October afternoon and Verdi Street smelled of burning leaves. It seems the notary'd always been talking about his first wife, especially at table, and what a wonderful cook she'd been. And Senyora Rosalia, who at first had followed the conversation and felt sorry her husband was so tormented by his memories, one day realized that she was nothing but a stick for him to lean on. She said as soon as he went off to work, she'd burst into tears and the "O my Gods" those walls had heard would melt a heart of stone. But more than complaining about how he made her cry, she complained about not being able to weep alone with all those smiling portraits of Rosalia spying on her. And how, in order not to see them, she'd learned to live without looking. She spoke, listened or kept quiet gazing off into the distance. So much worrying every day had aged her quickly so the corners of her mouth sagged and there were lines between her brows. All the time we were in her house she kept glancing at the clock and said it was a bad habit she'd picked up from her husband, who couldn't spent ten minutes without checking the time. She was wearing a gold medallion and in the middle was a little man's head with big eyes so full of black that only a speck of white was showing. Every time she looked at the clock she turned that medallion like she didn't notice what she was doing. A while later she'd turn it again so the face was showing. She wouldn't let that man's head live in peace.

The notary had left her with a daughter. Two years earlier she'd married her to a guy who worked in a bank and who'd spent the whole war hiding in a relative's attic. They had an eight-month-old baby boy, and when we arrived the daughter had just gone upstairs because the baby had woken up. Senyora Rosalia showed us onto the porch, where we sat down, and the garden looked very strange through all those colored panes. It looked like a false garden through the white ones. Senyora Rosalia told us she'd put some goldfish in the fountain but the cat had eaten them so she couldn't show them to us. A cat as nasty as a hyena who'd suddenly grab a fish and gobble it up in the kitchen. Then she said her daughter had deserved better, to marry some rich man, but she'd had to take what she could get because she wasn't getting any younger and none of her boyfriends seemed like the marrying type. It's true the bank employee was properly brought up, because to work in a bank you have to be upright and careful with money, which is how you can have something to live on when they take you out—not the bank directors, the passing years. We got up and went upstairs.

The daughter was waiting at the head of the stairs. She had very dark, close-set eyebrows and very thin lips. She wasn't wearing stockings and flopped around in her slippers and when she turned away I saw her heels, which looked like wax.

The bedroom stank and the kid was bawling in a fluffy cradle with pleats and a mosquito net over it. She stuck a pacifier in his mouth and the boy spat it out, and every time she stuck it in he spat it out. The daughter sat down, wiped her arms with a handkerchief, her mother handed her the child and the daughter took out a breast whiter than death and covered with veins. She squeezed it and a jet of what looked like pus squirted out. I turned away because the middle of her breast was all purple. The smell of milk mixed with the smell of wet sheets and Senyora Rosalia, after watching the baby suck for a while, started changing the sheets on the cradle and saying she'd hang the old ones out to dry on the balcony because they weren't dirty yet. She saw me looking at some dirty socks and kicked them under the bed. The kid was gasping and the daughter said she had to rest. She yanked her breast out of his mouth, tucked it away, pulled out the full one, and the kid grabbed it and started gagging again. He gagged silently, with his eyes bugging out of his head and all his blood in his face.

The husband arrived unexpectedly and Senyora Rosalia took him outside because she said he'd distract the baby. As soon as he was gone, she took a bottle of cologne and rubbed it all over her daughter's head and shoulders. Her son-in-law was blond, with hair that started way back from his forehead. A forehead that never ended. When they let him in again, he said he'd had a vision while he was totting up some figures. A kind of smoke. Senyora Rosalia immediately said she'd get the lenses changed on his glasses. He said no, what he'd seen bounced up and down like it was dangling on a wire from the ceiling and all of a sudden it had touched the floor and disappeared. The daughter pulled the baby off her breast and the bank employee asked if we'd mind him taking off his jacket. Senyora Rosalia said "Now we'll leave you two alone," and as we were going toward the stairs she said when a husband comes home from work he likes to tell stuff to his wife. They looked at each other like we weren't there. Like dead people's eyes. All pupils, motionless.

The street lights were on by the time we left. As we were walking home I decided never to get married.

_9 **XII** ONE DAY I TOLD PAULINA THAT A LONG TIME ago I'd seen a horse with a big skinless patch on its backside, swarming with flies. And I remembered it because that horse had such sad eyes. She said she'd never noticed horses' eyes but she paid a lot of attention to people's and how women's eyes would look dull if they didn't make them up. She said one day we'd paint our eyes and go out for a walk with lots of mascara on so people would enjoy looking at us.

We did it one day when Senyora Magdalena had gone to

the dentist because the root of one of her teeth was growing and jutting out the roof of her mouth. We took a cork
and a box of matches out to the tool shed. Paulina cut a
strip of cork, sharpened it like a pencil, and I lit a match
and burned one end of what was left of the cork. Then we
dipped the pencil in the black, made our eyes up and
thickened our eyebrows. My eyes were stinging by the
time we got outside. We walked down the street and my
heart was pounding just to think of the look on the first
person's face who saw me with those eyes like a lady's. It
was a man with one wooden leg and one real one, and he
walked by without looking at us. Then came two ladies
loaded down with baskets and an old lady with a younger
one beside her, who also didn't notice us. But a boy, who
must have been a student because he had books under his
arm, stopped in front of us and said our faces needed
washing. Paulina shoved him so hard that his books fell to
the ground. We ran up Verdi Street, yelling and holding
hands. As we turned into Camellia Street, we saw a kid
making mud pies; I picked up a handful and stuck it on
Mrs. Rius's wall.

I remember all this so well and I'm describing it because
that was the same day I saw Eusebi again. After so many
years. I was eating an apple Paulina'd given me and all of a
sudden I heard a whistle outside the gate. The garden was
a swirl of branches and leaves, and from far away came a
wave of memories: the ferris wheel, the fireworks, pine
needles, a marble with colored and clear streaks rolling
down a stony, dusty path. It was two years since the war

and Eusebi, outside the gate, tall and skinny, with his shirt unbuttoned and his hair badly cut, with that curl on his forehead, had become a man. I turned and walked over to the gate, hardly knowing what I was doing, and without saying a word I pressed my face against the bars. He touched my dimples. A few days later we started going out together. I was restless and didn't feel like going to bed when it was time or getting up once I was in it. I remember a path with hard-packed dirt and an agave with flowers like Canterbury bells and the sun setting behind it. One night he took me to his shack—his brother had died in the war—and I never went home again. And it was like the house and the people who'd taken me in, with those cups of lime-flower tea and the tower and the yellow easy chair and that business about the safety pin and the scrap of paper were in one of those stories they tell kids to scare them on winter nights or to make them happy, depending on what they're like. Paulina saw us leave.

XIII THE SHACK HAD TWO SOLID WALLS; THE others were made of tin sheets with old boards and pieces of sack stuffed in the cracks. Eusebi told me he'd been very sick when he'd come home from the war and that's why it looked so run-down and he'd had a hard time getting rid of the people who'd been living there. The shack had no windows. The bed was against one of the tin walls because that way it was easier to fit in the table and chairs and a chest of drawers with drawers that were hard to open because the wood was swollen from the damp. And the wall beside that bed, which was a cot, had some tin sheets that didn't fit together so we plugged the crack with old rags. We slept by that crack when it was hot out, but as soon as it got cooler we rearranged the furniture because we were more comfortable against the wall made of cinderblocks. Till we got sick of always moving furniture around and just left it like it was. When I was alone I'd lie down on the bed, take the rags out of the crack, and look at the shack next door, which had a window and solid walls. Often there was a guy shaving in that window; he hung the mirror on the part that opened and depending on how he opened and closed the window the mirror would flash in my face. One day I did the same to him with a piece of mirror I'd found in the garbage. When Eusebi saw it he said that mirror would bring us back luck. When spring came, the guy in the next shack put a pot of flowering pansies on his windowsill. Soon, when we met outside or at the fountain, we started saying hello. I enjoyed looking at him so much, especially when he was beside those pansies, that one time when I was carrying a glass pitcher of water I stumbled and the pitcher fell and cracked. He was blond, with a sunken chest and very white skin. They told me he was a marble cutter, and for a long time whenever I looked at him through the crack at the head of the bed I'd see him making an angel like the ones in cemeteries. And headstones with curly letters and capital letters in gold. But he made his living as a plasterer and was always covered with white dust. Maybe he wasn't sad, but he sure acted like he was. Like everyone in those shacks except me and Eusebi, he spoke only Castilian, and that annoyed me a little.

Sometimes in the evening, the old man with the hens would drop by. He made the rounds of all the shacks, collecting greens and potato peels. He and Eusebi were great buddies; they'd spend all night playing cards and sometimes go off together and I never knew where they were. While they played cards I'd look through the crack and see my plasterer's window lit up. If there was no light in the window I couldn't sleep, wondering where that blond plasterer could be. And just like I'd spent days and days waiting for Eusebi to whistle outside the gate, in that shack I was always waiting to see the plasterer, even if it was just a glimpse when he threw the dishwater out the window.

On rainy days, if it rained hard, water would come in everywhere. The leaks in the house where I'd grown up could be plugged; Senyor Jaume would mix some cement in a tray and run around on the roof, plugging cracks here and there. But the leaks in that shack couldn't be fixed because the roof was made of all kinds of weird things: boards and bricks piled on top of each other, all held together with reeds and plaster. One afternoon I went to watch the cars going by and I suddenly remembered, like they'd rapped my memory with a hammer, about a silk rose I'd seen at Maria-Cinta's dressmaker's house, the one who'd made me that dress embroidered with cherries, and I didn't stop till I reached a department store to see if I could find one like it. While I was looking for the artificial flower counter I tripped over an umbrella lying on the floor. Without thinking I picked it up and walked out with it. Whenever it rained I'd tie it to the ceiling above the bed and the water would run off it. The handle was gold and the silk was purple.

XIV SENYORA MATILDE WAS FROM CARTAGENA and lived a few shacks down from us. I knew her because one morning she'd warned me that a hen was eating the passionflower that had sprung up all by itself outside our door. She'd had seven children: three, the oldest, had died in the war, and the other four, two boys and two girls, were scattered around the world, and she was always waiting for their letters, which she'd take around to all the shacks. She could read palms and imitate a fly. She'd rub her hands together like they were her front legs and run one hand along one arm and then the other with her arms outstretched, and then she'd rub her face real quick with her hands and her fingers half clasped. The day she asked to read my palm I let her because I wanted to know if I'd make love with that plasterer, but he didn't come up. She told me she couldn't see much because the lines of my palm hid the truth. Till she saw a star on my hand and laughed and read my cards, which she knew how to do too. She said I'd live in a house with roses, not in the windows but above the windows, roses that wouldn't be roses but statues of roses, like statues of people. And how one night I'd see a sad man beside a dead woman who was alive. And all this would really happen.

Our shack made you laugh, with umbrellas all over. Some were stolen; neighbors had given us the rest. But I never took the purple umbrella outside. I planted bluebells beside the door and to make sure no hens ate them I made a fence around them. At sunset I'd go out and look at them, and when they flowered I'd sometimes pick one and crush it between my fingers so it would dye them purple, even though it was blue. Often the plasterer would stop and ask me how the bluebells were doing. And since when he looked at me all of a sudden I felt shabbily dressed, I went to steal a blouse.

The department store smelled like varnish, like the trolleys, and the light made everyone's face look sickly. You could hear music and the ladies walked back and forth and rummaged through everything and then sifted through it again, looking and looking. Blouses were piled on one counter: pink and blue. And white. They were stacked so all you saw was the neck and two front buttons, and the necks were pretty because there was a collar. While the girl who sold them, dressed in black with earrings like gold balls, showed one to a very well-dressed lady with a huge bust, I started fingering them and took one and half unfolded it and then folded it up again as though I hadn't liked it. I made sure no one was watching me. The salesgirls were busy selling stuff, but at the next counter there was a very young one who was painting her nails red. While I was waiting for her to finish polishing them and turn away, I went over to the slip counter. The music stopped and they put on another record that made me sleepy. But first, a very loud voice said everyone should go buy toothbrushes, which were on sale. I hardly even looked at the artificial flowers. The roses weren't silk and the filaments and buds in the middle of the red ones were too yellowish and coarse. When I went back to the blouses I saw another girl combing her hair next to the one polishing her nails.

The well-dressed lady still hadn't found anything she liked, and on the mezzanine, leaning over the railing and making faces at the two girls, who looked at each other and giggled from time to time, there was a soldier with a moustache. I still don't know how it happened, but suddenly I found myself out on the street with a blouse inside my jacket, rolled up in a ball. I'd grabbed my chance while the girls were giggling with that soldier, but I always figured he must have seen me. I knocked the blouse I liked off the counter, bent over to pick it up, and hid it.

It was tight around my chest. I put it on three days running and took it off again without daring to leave the shack. The fourth day, I made up my mind. I wore it kind of open, with the top three buttons undone. In the buttonhole on the collar I stuck a rose I'd plucked from a branch hanging over a wall. I went out just as the plasterer showed up. When he saw me he stopped and leaned his hand against the wall as high as he could reach so I was standing under that arm white with dust and fluff, also white. We looked at each other. After a while he said "Hello, Cecília," pulled a petal off the rose, stuck it between his teeth, which were white like a newborn puppy's, and slowly ate it. When nothing was left and he was about to pluck another, the old man with the hens walked by and said *"Buenos días y que aproveche."* The plasterer took his arm— I mean his hand—off the wall, and maybe without meaning to brushed it against my shoulder. I rushed back in our shack, but it was like all of me had stayed outside with that eaten rose petal and those bluebells.

That afternoon, a huge storm cloud spread over the shacks and at nightfall a wind blew up that seemed to come from the ground the way it swept everything up in the air. I went out, feeling worried because Eusebi still hadn't come home, and the first thing I saw was three or four umbrellas tumbling along with a crowd of kids behind them. There were lots of people outside; some women were yelling that we'd be flooded and the dogs were barking. The tin sheets on our roof were flying all over. Then it got dark as night. The rain, which had started with drops big as nickels every so often, started pouring down so hard that you could hardly walk through it. Some shacks were filling up with water. I was lucky because the plasterer and two women helped me weigh down the sheets that were left and catch the ones that had blown away. People ran by with straw baskets on their heads, and one woman stopped and spent a long time telling me how her mattress looked like a raft. Finally I was all alone with the plasterer, soaked from head to toe, and when that terrible lightning bolt flashed I saw we were staring at each other, that we'd been staring at each other for a long time in the dark. Then came the thunder, and it sounded like the earth was splitting. Then he leaned close to me and told me he loved me.

◆ **XV** IT TOOK US TWO WEEKS TO FIX WHAT THE WIND and rain had wrecked. The first few days all the paths were like muddy swamps, but just when it seemed like the storm had cooled things off, a heat wave struck. The sun beat down cruelly and the muddy streets turned into rivers of dust. The light was blinding, white and shimmery. One evening I don't know what happened. Everyone was feeling good, but with a kind of jumpy excitement. There was a crowd of girls with bare legs and loose hair kidding around by the fountain. I was waiting my turn with the plasterer, whose name was Andrés, and a girl named Tere, who was a big joker, stuck her thumb against the faucet and sprayed a man who was walking by with his jacket over his arm. The man lost his temper and was about to belt her, but while he was yelling another girl got him even wetter and he went away making a long speech to himself while everyone laughed so hard they must have heard us up in Heaven. Andrés, who hadn't said anything for a while, suddenly whispered in my ear that the summer was nice *con trigo y amapolas* and I was so busy listening that I didn't notice Eusebi till he was right in front of me with that cracked pitcher. Then Tere sprayed us and when Andrés, who hadn't noticed anything either, took my arm to pull me away, Eusebi, who was hopping mad, brought the pitcher down on his head. Some girls screamed. Andrés's shirt was stained with blood, and Eusebi led me away with an empty pitcher and a heart full of gloom.

Neither of us slept that night; we kept tossing and turning, and when we were tired of lying on one side we'd roll over on the other, but since we always turned at once either face to face or back to back, it was every man for himself and when the sun came up neither of us had slept a wink. Eusebi went out without a word; that evening, after trying all day to figure out whether I should do it, I went to visit Andrés. He was sleeping. I went up to the window with the pansies; some of them were still open, yellow and blue, but a lot had dried up and gone to seed. I looked over at my shack, which seemed very run-down with its rusty tin and faded umbrellas. I lit a fire. Andrés's forehead was hot and the bandage on his shoulder was soaked with blood. Senyora Matilde came to take care of him and was very surprised to see me. She had bandages and cotton. The cut was deep and inflamed, with a ring of pus around it.

When I left a half-hour later, Eusebi was waiting outside our door. Someone must have told him what I'd been up to, and even though he'd seen me come out, he asked where I was coming from. I told him I'd been taking care of Andrés. And I don't know what came over me, what kind of sadness, but I pulled up the bluebells so I wouldn't see any more flowers and then made supper and after supper I put on that blouse I'd stolen and stuck my finger in the buttonhole where the rose had been—I don't know why—and lay down on the bed with my face toward Andrés's shack. Early the next morning, when the sky was still dark, I tiptoed out and went to the fountain, turned on the faucet, drank some water and splashed a little on my face. The handle from the pitcher was lying on the ground. I took it home and hung it by the head of the bed.

The next day I went back to take care of Andrés. I went there every day for a whole week. After taking care of him I'd sit down at the foot of the bed and look at him. I'd hold his hand and since it was cooler, I could tell the fever was going down and we'd sit like that, him giving me his hand and me holding it. And those times around sunset, with people coming home to their shacks and the smell of frying food and green wood, everything, Andrés and me and the shack, was like a piece of candy. Two flies trapped alive in a piece of candy. One evening before I left, I bent over Andrés and he looked at me like a dog looks at his master and I kissed him on the cheek. I ran out and plucked a bluebell that had survived by some miracle, I sniffed it and buried my nose in it, where the blue starts to fade, so I could smell something tender.

XVI THE MOMENT I LEFT OUR SHACK AND PICKED up two pails of water I'd left in the sun for washing myself, I saw the old man with the hens. I'd started to hate him because he was a pest and stuck to me like a leech. He said he'd just had his hair cut and asked if they'd done a good job, because he was sure that when they'd held that little mirror behind his head he'd seen a lot of bare patches. He hadn't dared to complain because he and the barber were good friends and the barber always said he knew his trade inside out. I put down the pails and when I raised my head I saw the fly on his pants, which sagged below his belly and seemed held up by some miracle. To get rid of him I said it looked fine. He was a guy who walked and talked slowly, swaying a little like he was still on deck, because he'd worked for years in the merchant marine. He told me he'd known a barber in Manila who'd done a really good job, and since I didn't answer him he started in with that story, which even the kids knew by heart, about two white whales leaping in and out of the water like they were playing for two days and two nights.

I left him with the words still in his mouth and went off to the bathhouse with my two pails. The bathhouse was a patch of ground with a wooden fence around it, shorter than a person, and if whoever was washing didn't bend down a little, people would see your head from outside. Some sacks made a curtain that covered the entrance and vines with thin leaves were climbing the planks. In the summer it was great for pouring water over yourself so you'd be clean and could cool off a little.

I pulled my dress over my head and draped it over the planks, half outside and half inside but within reach because sometimes when a girl was washing some jerk would take her clothes. It was a cloudy sunset and a breeze rustled the grass, which was already turning yellow. I ladled some water over myself and started soaping with an esparto glove and as I was doing my belly I heard Andrés's voice nearby asking if he could help me. I bent over in a hurry, because from far away you could only see the head on the person inside but from close up you could see their whole body. And then I suddenly felt like laughing, a mean laugh from deep inside, thinking how mad Eusebi would get if he saw Andrés cured, standing next to me, and me in my birthday suit. I squeezed up against the boards and told him if he didn't peek I'd let him rinse me off and to come to the entrance, where I'd hand him the pails and ladle. Through the crack between the sacks he gave me a little pink flower, and I stuck it in my hair.

He started pouring water over me and the air and water smelled like sun and he poured water on my shoulders; and the edge of the ladle, just once and maybe by accident, brushed my skin. But then I stopped laughing and my chest, which was already a little tight, got much tighter because I heard Eusebi screaming at Andrés like a nut that if he didn't beat it he'd slit his belly open like a pig's. Andrés didn't answer and I crouched over, freezing because everything had suddenly turned cold. I heard them arguing and when it sounded like they were far away, I put on my dress without drying myself and ran back to our shack. Eusebi was waiting outside. He kicked my ass so hard I didn't stop till I reached the bed, and then he came and tore my dress off. I didn't know if he wanted to make love or murder me, but after standing there thinking with the dress in one hand he suddenly opened the trunk, threw the dress inside, and locked it. Then he dragged the trunk outside and left, yelling that now I'd stay put. I didn't know what he wanted; I thought maybe he was planning to rip up the few clothes I had and I felt like crying, because they've always made me cry every time I felt like laughing.

A while later Senyora Matilde knocked, all upset; she pounded so hard the whole place shook. She said Andrés and Eusebi were killing each other at the fountain and I should go and try to break it up. I told her I couldn't leave because I was naked and Eusebi had taken all my clothes. She said I should wrap a sheet around myself and get moving as fast as I could; and even so I might not be in time. And I would have died right there, so confused I didn't know which way to turn, if Eusebi hadn't stormed in saying he'd beaten up Andrés, giving him a sock that had left him flat as a pancake and if I wanted to see him I'd find him lying beside the fountain.

ঙ **XVII** TWO MONTHS AFTER THOSE FIGHTS THE COPS came and took Eusebi away. Along with the old man with the hens. They came early one morning and gave him just time to dress, and even so they made him do it right in front of them. Before they left I went up to him with my mouth dry. I offered him my cheek and he kissed it. Then I said goodbye to him in a voice I could hardly recognize. And when they were barely fifty steps away I felt like I shouldn't stay in that shack, that I shouldn't let him leave in that dead early morning light, so little between those big cops. I started running because they were almost out of sight. He was walking between two of them behind the old man with the hens, who was between two others. When I'd practically caught up with them I tripped and fell to my knees in the dust. I got up, scared I'd lost them, and for a moment I couldn't see them but then they reappeared from behind a pile of old cars. I stopped in front of a café just outside the shantytown, because they all got in a van and disappeared down the street like they'd never existed. I sat down on the edge of a barrel with a plant in it. Drops of blood oozed from my knee because gravel had gotten under the skin.

Senyora Matilde knew things I'd never heard about. She told me the old man was a thief who'd been thrown out of the merchant marine and climbed over people's walls and broke into their houses. I'd always thought the little bit of money Eusebi made came from watching cars outside theaters or carrying suitcases in train stations. But Senyora Matilde opened my eyes, saying they stole water meters from outside houses and manhole covers and all the bronze they could pry off statues. And tools from construction sites if the watchmen didn't look sharp or fell asleep. They had a wheelbarrow they rented from the owner of the café. One day Tere's mother had seen them pushing it along and it was piled so high with tools that they had trouble moving it.

Because of all that stealing, they put him in jail. Everyone told me I should do something to get him out. I didn't know which jail they'd taken him to but several people I knew around the shantytown said I should write to them all. I wrote and no one answered. Then they told me to go see the civil governor. I spent lots of nights imagining I was in front of him and trying to think what I should say. He'd be sitting behind a big desk with a light with a green shade and next to the light a photo of his wife and kids, all looking at him while he sat back in a big black leather chair, with his hands folded over his belly, as if he was about ready to be laid in his coffin. And me lying in bed, imagining myself standing before that governor and I was sure my mouth would clamp shut when it came time to tell him Eusebi was in jail and ask him tó let him out.

They found clothes so the governor could see people in our shantytown were human beings too. Tere lent me a suit with a jacket that was too tight and a pair of pink shoes that were too big. Another girl who liked me a lot gave me some cotton gloves, the right one with a rusty crease across the palm. Andrés told me to stay put and not go see the governor. Tere's boyfriend said I should wear a white rose in my hair and a fat lady who was listening and who nobody'd ever seen before said it should be a red one. But everyone said I had to have a flower in my hair because deep down inside the governor was a man like any other and a girl like me would leave him with his mouth hanging open. Someone said I should go just as I was and try to make him feel sorry for me instead of getting all dolled up. Finally they found a straw hat somewhere. It was a little worn and I hid it a few days later and said I couldn't remember where I'd put it. Because God knows what I looked like with it on.

Lots of times I'd make up my mind and get dressed, saying I was going to see the governor, and then just wander around the streets. I liked looking at the liqueur ads in bar windows; some were very pretty, with well-drawn letters, two or three colors, and pictures. When I saw the bottles inside, lined up in front of the mirror, I thought how Eusebi was locked up and I had to get him out. One day I stopped at the gate to the park and stood there looking at the trees and grass, unable to go in even though all that greenery soothed me. Another day I went down a very narrow street with lots of washing hung out to dry and dripping water. You could hardly see the sky. But I thought how Eusebi could see even less through his bars. On the corner was a building with bulging walls. I would have given anything to see it cave in. It was Red Street and it stayed fixed in my memory. I liked all the streets: Fishermen's Street, Salt Street, Sea Street. I walked around dressed up while sailors and stevedores whistled at me. Sometimes I'd stop in front of the building where the governor had his office and look at it like it was a theater set and think how the governor in his black leather chair had no idea there was someone at the entrance who wanted to ask him to free a prisoner. But right afterward I felt sure I'd never go in. Because I was afraid of two things: first, that one of my shoes would fall off, and second, that when the governor asked me the prisoner's name and I said Eusebi, a servant in hose would come and push me back out into the street.

⁂ **XVIII** I STAYED AT ANDRÉS'S PLACE TILL FINALLY I was living with him. Almost without wanting to, and when I didn't like him so much anymore. We stored things in my shack and lived in his, which had cinderblock walls and a roof that didn't leak. Lots of Sundays we'd go down to the sea and look at the salt water and beds of mussels and the colors from the setting sun. Sometimes the water would ripple like it was nervous and the sun, before setting, would streak it yellow, the color of mussels inside, pale when they're raw and oranger when they're cooked. With black ribbons that half hide those little knobs that look like noses. One afternoon, I asked Andrés to take me to the cemetery. He stared at me horrified and I didn't dare tell him that when Eusebi and I were kids we went there all the time and how Eusebi had seen dead people burning like flames on candles and how once he'd wanted me to spend the night there with him and I'd refused to do it. As usual, we walked around the harbor and saw lots of sailors as if the sea had too many and was washing them ashore. Some had come down a gangplank with swaying ropes on each side and they strolled around, looking happy and holding hands, with those wide pants flapping around their shoes. Two officers had also come ashore. One was blond and had gold braid on his cap. When he passed me he looked, and to get a better look he stopped long enough to think something nasty. Luckily Andrés had bent over and didn't notice him. When he stood up he told me to keep quiet, that he'd found something pretty. When we got home he showed me a glass heart on a little chain with a broken clasp. I still remember it so well because a few days after finding that glass heart, Andrés began to cough a lot. It's true that I'd started living with him when I wasn't so attracted to him anymore, I mean when seeing him didn't make my heart pound, but now I started liking him a whole lot, from right up close, and it was like he was dying and he told me how since the day I'd asked him to rinse me off he hadn't had five minutes' peace, as if some wicked god had sentenced him to think of nothing but me. He talked about the nights he'd spent staring at our shack because I was inside it and how sometimes he'd have thoughts of love and see me coming out of the shack, but it wasn't really me, it was just an illusion, and when I was by his side and he embraced me he'd wake up from his dream and find it was just the night that he'd embraced. He always said those kinds of things, which gave me goosebumps.

Soon he began to cough up blood. And five months after the glass heart and the first cough he died, consumed by fever and with eyes as big as saucers. The women made a ring around me so I wouldn't see them take him away. But Senyora Matilde told me the horses were black. The neighbors gave me the money for his burial.

Tere, who did piecework for a factory, told me I could make a living sewing shirtwaist blouses. To do one quickly you had to put it in the machine without pinning it. They gave me the pieces. First I had to make the collars and sew them on the neckbands; then the cuffs and the seams along the sides. Then I sewed up the sleeves, put the cuffs on the sleeves, sewed the sleeves to the body and finally did the buttons and made the buttonholes by hand. Senyora Matilde lent me a sewing machine she'd bought cheap from the old man with the hens. The brand was White, U.S.A., and it worked with a treadle. Tere showed me where to oil it and gave me an oil can. She showed me how to thread the needle. The pay was average, but you had to do six a day to eat and I only got up to three. I did the first one as best I could and everything came out crooked but Tere said she'd sneak it by her boss mixed in with the others. The machine had its good and bad days. On the bad ones, the thread got tangled in the seams and made loops. When I cut them everything came undone like it had never been sewed. *"Paciencia,"* Tere'd say, *"ya aprenderás a dominar la máquina."* Once one of the holes on the belt ripped: the hole a wire had gone through that fastened the two ends. I pumped the treadle but the wheel wouldn't turn and the needle wouldn't go up or down. After thinking it over for a while, I cut off the end with the torn hole and made a new hole with a nail I had to hammer because the belt was so hard. When I'd made the hole I ran the wire through it and flattened it against the belt, but I'd been stupid because when I hooked up the belt I only ran it around the big wheel and I should have run it around the little one too—that is, around both of them. I had to dig out the wire with a knife because I'd got it so tight against the belt, and then I did run the belt around both wheels and hooked the wire in again. I oiled the whole belt because since I'd cut off that piece with the hole it was a little short and taut. When everything was set, the needle broke. Tere lent me one of hers, but it was too short and didn't catch the thread coming from the shuttle. After hunting all over, I found one that worked all right, and in the store where I bought it they told me I was lucky they had it and it was the last one because that machine belonged in a museum. When I put the needle in, the wheel wouldn't turn. Tere had a repairman come who was a friend of hers. He came at eight one Sunday morning and when I saw him I thought an angel had come to visit me. He was blond, like that officer the day with the glass heart, and he had curls that hung down in a kind of way that reminded me of Eusebi, and I felt like crying. He just glanced at the machine; then he squatted down by the wheel and said I'd have to change the wire because I needed that piece of belt I'd had to cut off on account of the torn hole. When he'd put a longer wire in he told me to try the machine. I sat down and worked it slowly, but the thread bunched up and made loops. Then he took the belt off the wheel and lifted the top. I'd never looked inside the machine and I watched the shuttle go, shiny and sharp, darting back and forth like a mad hornet. Without closing it, he knelt next to the wheel and his head brushed against my skirt. He spent a couple of hours trying to figure the machine out; every now and then he'd tap it with a hammer, he oiled it, his head brushed against my skirt again and he said "Excuse me." When he was done, the machine worked again. I asked how much I owed him and he said it was a favor. I never saw him again, but I'd fallen in love, and the seams all came out crooked and I couldn't stop thinking about that repairman and those curls on his forehead. I got up to four blouses a day but I was starving and I couldn't walk because my stomach and leg muscles ached so much. I slept curled up with my fists clenched and when I opened my eyes, even if it was still dark, the first thing I saw was that machine like some ferocious animal. And one night, without thinking, I dragged it outside the shack, picked up my purse, and, skinny as a rail, went out looking for men on the Rambles.

XIX WITH MY PURSE OVER MY ARM AND OLD clothes on, I watched the ones who were better dressed and more determined than me. I wasn't good at hooking men. The worst thing was that I'd fall in love at first sight with guys I'd never see again. And if I didn't fall in love, that was even more awful because deep inside there'd be a kind of ache for that man who didn't attract me and who was all alone. I'd rather not describe how ashamed I felt opening my purse and slipping the money in. Senyora Matilde said I shouldn't do it, that I'd lose my looks right away, that I should have gone on sewing because if I'd kept on I would have ended up making enough to live on and buy myself a new machine.

A few months later I got pregnant and Senyora Matilde gave me an abortion with just a sprig of parsley to let some air in. They had to take me to the hospital. When I got out I wanted to know what it had been because in the evenings, surrounded by sick people, that's all I ever thought about. Boy or girl. It seems you couldn't tell because it hadn't grown enough to see. Senyora Matilde said she'd dug a hole a little outside the shantytown and gone at night with it in a pail to bury it. She'd dumped it out of the pail and packed down the earth and then put a big stone on top with a little one on it so she'd know where it was buried and no dog could dig it up. I walked out that way and didn't see any big stone with a little one on top of it, but I picked up any old stone and dropped it in my purse.

They preached to me a lot, but even though I knew it was stupid I went back to the Rambles. The first day was dreadful. When I got there, I just stood around for a long time, staring at the clock on the opera house. Since no one spoke to me, I got the urge to go to the park entrance and smell the trees and grass, and when I was there I decided to go see if that bulging wall on the corner of Red Street was still standing. And right at the entrance to Red Street, a guy who looked a little like Eusebi snatched my purse and ran off with it. I chased him but he was faster and got away. Miserable, I wandered back to the park and started crying, and a while later a sailor tried to comfort me and asked why I was so sad. He told me he was on shore leave and was from Majorca. He took me back to his hotel; the room was small and looked out on a narrow street. He kept me locked up for three days. Sometimes he'd calm down and look out the window, whistling under his breath, but when he got worked up he'd say "You're mine, mine," and he said he'd take me to live surrounded by water, which was when I started getting scared, because it terrified me to live surrounded by water, surrounded by the sea. He said he had a house so white you couldn't look straight at it. The third night, frightened out of my wits, I managed to sneak out while he was sleeping. Without a cent, because since we were going to get married. . . .

The next morning my tongue was thick and I felt very upset. I didn't know what I wanted. I went out that night, a rainy night, and that was the night I spent with that distinguished gentleman, in a huge bed with lots of goldfish with fringy tails in a tank at the head of the bed. I couldn't stop looking at all the pretty things and felt a little embarrassed with my muddy shoes and no stockings. But that gentleman seemed very kind and pretended not to notice. While I was undressing I looked at his cufflinks. Cufflinks with blue stones, almost black, that flashed when he moved them like they were lit up inside. I was about to ask him to let me see them up close, but I didn't dare. Afterward, when we'd been resting for a while, he asked why I was holding his hand. I opened my eyes, and since I didn't know what to answer, I said, laughing, that it was so he'd never leave me and I could keep him forever. When he got up he stuck his finger in the dimple on my cheek, turned it like he was trying to make it deeper, and went to wash. Toward midday I started feeling as upset as the day before and began to look around the shack. I didn't know what I was hunting for. There was something I needed to breathe and I didn't know what or where it was. It took me hours to remember, and when I finally did, it was like I'd known it all along without realizing I knew, as if part of my brain was asleep. I was looking for the hairpin with the stars, as though I'd worn it the day before, but I hadn't seen it for the longest time and had no idea where it was. I went out to buy another and couldn't find any in the trimming shops or department stores. Halfway up the Rambles I stopped in my tracks, scared stiff, because I saw a sailor who looked like the one who wanted to take me to Majorca. I walked up the Rambles and the Passeig de Gràcia, thinking all the time the sailor was behind me, till I felt very tired and sat down on a bench. I must have been a little feverish because my forehead was hot and my lips were dry. A white car went by slowly with a girl inside it; it seemed like it was gliding above the ground. I closed my eyes and a strange joy came over me. I thought someday I'd have a car too and sit in the back with a pearl necklace and pearl earrings and a ring with a white pearl and a black one and the chauffeur would open the door for me and say "miss" with his cap in his hand. And I'd be wearing a pink dress.

I must have dozed off. After a while I felt something brush against my leg and woke up with a start because at first I didn't know what it was. There was a little girl standing in front of me, staring and sucking her thumb. I leaned over and touched the tip of her nose, but she ran off toward a lady dressed in black with white hair who was talking with two well-dressed gentlemen. I got up, and it was only then that I realized I was almost outside the building where Maria-Cinta had lived. Maria-Cinta . . . I hadn't thought of her in a long time and at that moment it was like she was standing in front of me. Tall and pretty, dressed in white, with two black foxes around her neck, like the last day I'd seen her. I couldn't resist going up to her apartment and seeing if she still lived there. I meant to ask the doorman but my legs carried me past him. On the landing, outside her door, stood a girl holding a big bouquet. When she heard me she turned around, looked at me awhile, and suddenly cried "Cecília!" in a voice that made me jump. It was Paulina. Just then the door opened and Paulina handed the flowers, which were irises, to a chambermaid and told her to tell Senyora Carolina she'd come back another day, that she was in a hurry and couldn't stay. We went down the stairs together. We stopped at the front door, there were tears in her eyes, and she said she'd always thought a lot about me. That she'd recognized me right away. A leaf fell from a plane tree. I said "Look, a leaf," and I don't know why but I started laughing hysterically. And we hugged each other.

XX FINALLY WE GOT ON A BUS. WE'D WALKED ALL the way up the Carrer Gran lost in conversation, she asking questions and me answering them, and we were tired. We got off at the foot of Mount Carmel, at the start of a winding path. Paulina's house was halfway up the hill. You went through a little green wooden gate and the garden climbed the hill on both sides of some stone steps with rows of young cypresses along them. The garden was closed off on the left and right by two other rows of cypresses planted very thickly, and beyond the cypresses, the hill was covered with purple irises. On the way she'd told me how Maria-Cinta had died in a hospital where no one came to see her, not even Senyora Magdalena and Senyor Jaume. She'd had an accident that had left her with a bad break in one leg and something wrong inside her. Her lover, Maria-Cinta hadn't told anyone for a long time, had been shot during the war on the Arrabassada. Paulina'd visited her in the hospital and brought her chocolates when she had some. She'd said she prayed to die quickly because men weren't interested in lame women, and no man would love her because they didn't know what she'd been like as a little girl or how her parents had held their breath so they wouldn't give her a cold. When they buried her the apartment came up for rent, and Paulina, who heard about it from Senyor Jaume, told Senyora Carolina. She'd been her first mistress and had been looking for a place since the war because it scared her to live in a house. Paulina, who still liked her a lot, went to see her and brought her irises from time to time. And that's how we met. She didn't know anything about Raquel.

We sat down outside, in front of the house, in two wicker chairs facing each other. She told me that house belonged to her lover, a gentleman from Tarragona who had a cannery and who, when he visited her, liked for her to dress up as a chambermaid. She told me about Mrs. Rius's youngest son. They'd lived together for quite a while on Floridablanca Street. Before she hadn't liked him; it was the oldest one she'd liked. But one day, not long after I'd run away from home, two cops had come for him. Not because he'd done anything wrong, but because he'd been seeing some people who were in hiding. They only kept him in jail a couple of months but even though it sounds ridiculous he came back a changed man. He'd stopped acting so wild and looked so sad it would have broken your heart. When they started living together there were lots of quarrels in the family because he'd fallen in love with the maid. And they had to split up. She said she wasn't very attracted to the gentleman from Tarragona because he was so old and fat; but she could rely on him. We got up and stood looking over toward Tibidabo. It was a mild afternoon without the slightest breeze, and the garden was calm and still. Suddenly I noticed that she was staring at me as if she wanted to look deep inside me; I don't know what she expected me to say. To distract her, I asked her to show me the flowers on the other side of the house that you couldn't see from where we were. There were a few rosebushes and white irises growing among the rocks. She told me that in the afternoon, when she was bored, she planted irises. Because in the afternoons, when she'd finished her housework, all kinds of things went through her head. And bothered her. She told me that irises grew by themselves, like grass, and she'd cover that whole stretch of hill with them, but she had to plant a lot because sometimes women in rags would come from the other side of the hill and steal bunches. She'd picked a white iris for me; I held it, not knowing what to do, and the petals shook because I was shook up myself. I told her I'd made blouses, that I'd lived for a long time with that guy she'd liked so much but they'd arrested him because he and his pal were thieves and I hadn't heard from him since. Not even where he was. How afterward I'd lived with a plasterer who'd died young, coughing up blood. I told her if I hadn't stopped sewing I don't know what would have happened and that

for the time being I was working the Rambles. That bothered her a lot and she said it couldn't go on, that if I
wanted she'd talk to the gentleman from Tarragona and see
if he had some friend who'd like a girl he could count on.
The iris had three petals that drooped and then turned upward. And in the distance Tibidabo was turning blue.

Paulina's house was high and narrow, built up against a
hill; the first floor had a dining room and a kitchen, upstairs there was a living room and a little terrace, and the
third floor had a bathroom and bedroom that looked out on
a street they were still paving. Above the chairs in the garden in front of her house there was a trellis that went from
two columns to the railing around the terrace. There were
three plants: a passionflower, a grapevine, and a wisteria.
The grapevine was old, the passionflower had taken root
by itself like that one outside our shack, and the wisteria
caught your eye because its trunk was covered with leaves
and shoots and then there'd be a bare patch like a dead
root and then suddenly another with all those leaves cast-
ing shadows. She stared at me again with that look that
made me uncomfortable and said "You're a princess." And
how she and Mrs. Rius had always said so and everyone
had said I was a princess. We stood there for a while together without saying anything. When I was ready to go
she said she'd pick me a bouquet of irises. I said no, she'd
just be wasting them.

◈ XXI THE DAY AFTER THAT BUSINESS WITH PAULINA

and the irises, Senyora Matilde came to my shack looking
very worried and saying she'd seen the old man with the
hens in the distance. I was petrified and the first thing I
thought was Eusebi must have died. The old man with the
hens came by early that evening looking very calm. His
head was shaved and he was so skinny he could hardly
stand. He came into the shack like it bothered him to see
it and stood there slowly shaking his head for a while. The
first thing he told me was I'd done the right thing and Eusebi was a jerk and the best thing I could do was get him
out of my head if he was still in there. I asked him what
had happened. He said don't worry, it was nothing, and all
in all he'd been lucky. I could see he didn't feel like talking
and I had to pry every word out of him. It seems Eusebi
had tried to escape a few times but they'd always caught
him and every time they caught him they just about beat
him to a pulp. They'd beaten him so much that he was half
crazy and one day he suddenly knifed a guard in the back.
Luckily it didn't do much harm, but no one could find out
where he'd gotten the knife though they beat him a lot.
The worst thing was that when they were beginning to
think he was crazy someone found out he'd been on a com-
mittee during the war. I was surprised, because Eusebi always said he'd been a soldier and before that he'd been a
kid. When he'd finished talking, the old man scratched the
back of his neck and shook his head again and said *"Tiene
para años."* Then he asked if I could help him out. I took
out my change purse and gave him everything I had. He
left right away saying he had two or three more stops to

make. That night I had a very weird little dream that kept coming back afterward. There was a big stretch of plain with a dead tree on the left. At the foot of the tree was a baby in diapers who kept wiggling its arms. On the right, small because it was so far away, there was a dog that kept coming closer and closer to the baby but never got there. I woke up with tears in my eyes and on my cheeks. I guess I must have cried in my sleep.

I got up as usual but two hours later I felt so sick I had to go back to bed. I had a fever and all I could think about was Maria-Cinta, though I tried not to. That night Senyora Matilde came by and I told her everything the old man with the hens had said. She said I shouldn't complain because if they'd let Eusebi out he might have beaten me to death. I was sick for three weeks. Lots of times I'd feel like throwing up toward evening because I thought I was surrounded by irises. Senyora Matilde brought me saucepans of soup, but they made me sick and I'd throw them out at night. It killed me to think I'd have to go back to the Rambles. One day I decided to go out because I couldn't stand it anymore cooped up in that shack. I was still sick and bleeding a lot. I'd hardly eaten a thing since I'd seen the old man with the hens: a few pieces of bread and sometimes an apple from a basket Tere'd brought me. All that stuff about Eusebi had gotten me down, though at the time I felt like I'd gotten rid of something that was bothering me inside and sapping my strength without my knowing it. I walked up the Rambles to the Plaça de Catalunya and sat down on a bench wet with rain. I was thirsty and the white foamy water spouting from the fountain made me even thirstier. I don't know why, but I thought about Maria-Cinta and like in a trance I saw her coming toward me with that diamond cross on her neck and she took my hand and brought me home with her and I saw Eusebi tailgating on the car to see where we were going and I saw him outside the gate and they were beating him. . . . My hands and backbone were cold when I got up and I started walking slowly because I had a cramp in one leg. The sky had turned black and people hurried by. I went into a doorway and stayed there for a while till I got bored. I didn't know where to go. The thunderstorm caught up with me a little before Aragon Street. I didn't pay any attention and went on walking with my hands in my raincoat pockets while the water got under my collar and trickled down my back. I had to stop for a moment because my head was spinning. Cars went by splashing water on both sides and I could feel the water squishing in my shoes every time I took a step.

By the time I got to the park it had stopped raining but the sky was still gray. I sat down on a bench in front of two statues that were half lying down and I stayed there for a while with my mind a blank. When I got up my hair was plastered to my face and I didn't feel like myself. I was hungry, so hungry it hurt. I crossed the street and went into a big café on the corner. There was a high bar and everything behind it was chrome and glass. I chose a corner table, far from the window and near the bar. While I was waiting for the waiter to finish serving coffee to an old couple my teeth started chattering like they weren't mine.

All of a sudden I saw his white jacket beside me and to get up the strength to order a coffee and a ham sandwich I had to tell myself if I didn't eat I'd die. The waiter wiped the table with a little rag before setting down my order. I had to force myself to eat slowly because I felt like gulping everything down without chewing it. I could feel them watching me. There was a man sitting facing me at the end of the bar with a toothpick in his mouth. I felt even hungrier when I finished the ham sandwich and I ordered another.

I knew when it came time to pay I'd have to tell them I was broke. I'd known it when I came in, but as time went by I got more and more scared. Finally I had to tell them. The waiter told me to cut the crap, that I had to pay, that's all he needed and after telling me a few times he said it to the people at the bar. Another waiter appeared out of nowhere and then the boss came. I showed them my empty change purse and told them I'd been robbed. The other waiter started laughing hysterically and the boss, very politely but very firmly, told me to be good enough to pay. The other waiter said he'd already asked me twice and I had some nerve. I told him not to insult me, I hadn't paid because I couldn't, and he told me I was old enough to take care of myself. Then the boss suddenly stuck his face right next to mine and spattering me with spit shouted lady don't get smart with me or I'll have you locked up. I got mad and told him I wasn't a bit scared of the police, that I'd enjoy getting to know them and I wasn't a bit scared. The boss just shouted louder and louder about the coffee and the ham. The other waiter who didn't take it all that seriously started telling the whole story to a gentleman who'd just come in and was hanging up his raincoat. How if instead of refusing to pay I'd asked them nicely. The first waiter, who'd been talking to himself and waving his arms around like he wasn't all there, asked where I lived and I said it was none of his business but I'd tell him anyway to make him happy, that I lived in a shantytown. The boss gave me a nasty look and I started giving him nasty looks back. I guess he couldn't take it because he gave me a slap that just about knocked me down. Then I blew up and screamed that he'd hit me just because I was defenseless, that I'd been left in the street when I was little like a bag of garbage for the wind to scatter . . . without parents or brothers or sisters or anyone. . . . And I grabbed a glass off a table and threw it at his head. Then the real excitement started because two guys got in an argument over me. The gentleman who'd hung up his raincoat stepped in front of the boss and told him not to overdo it, that you couldn't blame people for being hungry, and my waiter who was still talking to himself threw his rag down in fury and a young man who was drinking Calisay said don't make such a fuss, that he'd pay for it himself and he couldn't believe they'd bother a beautiful dish like me over a squirt of coffee and a few scraps of ham. And he paid for me. As soon as he'd paid and turned around to sip his drink I felt someone touch my arm and say let's go. I turned to see who it was. The man who'd touched me had a cracked lip and through the crack you could see a gold tooth. It was the man with the toothpick. He had dark eyes and little hands, like they hadn't grown since he was fourteen. As we were walking out the young man with the Calisay said that's how it always was, the one who paid got left and the one who hadn't paid went off with the girl. And the boss, who was standing by the door holding it open, told the man with the tooth to watch out.

✒ **XXII** WE SEPARATED TO LET A WOMAN GO BY HOLDing a kid's hand and I lagged behind a little like I was following him. All of a sudden he turned around and I turned away to keep from seeing him and I saw a cake in a bakery window with almond flakes around the sides and frosting on top. He waited for me and we started walking again side by side like when we'd come out of the café. Everything was natural: the clouds breaking up so you could see patches of blue, the water flowing down the gutters and pouring into the sewers. Lots of people were waiting at the trolley stop and a little further away a woman with a bouquet was watching a girl come out of a notions store. My heart froze because I remembered when I was little I'd gone to that store a few times and maybe if I went in I'd find a hairpin like the one I'd lost. Two blocks past the trolley stop, the man with the toothpick said "Here we are." And we went into a restaurant. The lobby was small, there was just a counter and a staircase opposite the door but on the right, through a glass partition you could see a big room full of tables and chairs. We went upstairs, where there was a long, narrow dining room with a kitchen separated off by another counter with another glass partition that had a little door to pass food through; you could see them fixing it. The tables had paper tablecloths, with glasses turned upside down and little glass vases with paper cornflowers and poppies. At the end of that dining room were two doors: one led to a storeroom and the other to a bedroom with a glassed-in porch outside it with a sink and a few wires covered with clothespins. As we walked past I saw the cook peeling potatoes. He gaped at me with his knife in one hand and a potato in the other, like he'd never seen a woman before. In the bedroom, the restaurant owner told me to get undressed so they could dry my clothes. And he left. I crawled into bed, freezing, but first I washed my feet, one after the other, under the faucet in the sink. After quite a while the door opened as if by magic and a woman came in wearing an apron, tall and thin, with a wrinkled face longer than a horse's. She brought me a glass of milk with ladyfingers. I ate them all and drank the milk slowly so they wouldn't get mushy and stick in my throat. As soon as the woman had left with my wet clothes, I looked around. When I got tired of looking I settled down to sleep. I closed my eyes and opened them like I was playing at dozing off. Then I noticed an engraving on the wall in front of me with a frame made of gilded leaves. It showed a horse in profile with a ribbon around its tail. The man sitting on it was wearing a yellow coat the color of egg yolks, with a coffee-colored belt. I stayed there for a while, with one eye open and the other shut, looking at the color of the sky above the horse, grayish blue, and the mountains in the background, vague as moss and a few vague trees and everything so vague it dissolved, and I fell asleep.

When I woke up, the moonlight was coming through the balcony. I stretched and curled up, feeling thirsty for more milk and hungry for green almonds. The faucet in the sink was dripping. You could smell rancid oil and hear lots of voices talking. When the voices died down and the smell of oil was fading, the restaurant owner came in; I heard the switch click, and the three lights on the ceiling went on. As if he was alone, he put some notebooks on the table beneath the engraving and sat down so it looked like he was balancing his books. I didn't dare to breathe and thought maybe he'd forgotten me. After quite a while he got up and asked if I was sleeping. I said no, I was awake, and then he pulled his shirt over his head and told me he'd been born free and didn't want to get married because he was scared of having kids, that maybe he'd enjoy them but he didn't want to find out. That if he had them with me maybe he'd be banging his head against the wall. He didn't explain further and it seemed like he didn't even know what he was saying. That if I wanted to stay he wouldn't throw me out. He saw I was looking at the horse and told me he'd chosen that engraving himself. That his father's photo had been in that frame but he'd taken it out one day when he was in a bad mood; that he'd had to pull off six strips of masking tape, dig out little nails with a scissors, and then pull out three tight layers of cardboard before he could get at the photo. That when he finally held it in his hand he'd had trouble deciding what to do; all he'd wanted was to put it away but finally, in rage and sadness, he'd torn it up. He asked me like it was hard for him to get the words out if it was true what I'd said in that argument at the café, that I'd never known my parents. I said yes. And that's when he told me he'd never known his mother because he'd killed her being born.

&9 **XXIII** EUSEBI AND ANDRÉS HAD BOTH ATTRACTED me. I never felt attracted to that restaurant owner, whose name was Cosme. But I was hungry. The day I'd been there a month, he wanted to celebrate by drinking a bottle of champagne before bedtime. And every month on that same day we had to drink a bottle of champagne. Cosme wore a ring he never took off, even when he was washing or sleeping: a gold band with a row of diamonds and rubies. The gold was worn thin on the inside. He told me that ring was all he had from his mother. He didn't want me to wear makeup, and because of that we quarreled and he wouldn't give me a cent. I liked to put on makeup so I could look the same as other girls. It seemed like the cook had fallen in love at first sight. He stared and stared at me. He was thirty years old but no one would have guessed it because he was short and slim, all muscle, with a mouth from ear to ear and ears that looked a couple of sizes too big for him. He said his blood was thin, that the heat in the kitchen was bad for the red cells and when he looked at it under a microscope he'd bought at the flea market, all he saw was white cells. Without doing anything to bring it on, I had a miscarriage. Cosme acted sad; it seemed to get to him, though he'd never asked me to marry him. I looked paler than that cook's thin blood. I never found out if it was a boy or a girl. That was the first thing I asked Cosme when he came to visit me at the clinic. After looking at me a long time, he waved his hand in front of my eyes a few times and told me not to think about it any more. He made me promise.

Long before Midsummer Night Cosme said we'd go out and have some fun to get that miscarriage off my mind, and how he'd dress me up so I'd really shine. He took me to buy some black satin shoes with diamond horseshoes around the tops. He also came along when I bought my dress. Black satin. The dressmaker made it just like he ordered: with a high neck and long sleeves down to my wrists. They even had pointed flaps on the ends that hung down to my knuckles. A full-length skirt. He took the glass heart off my chain and replaced it with a gold and alabaster medallion showing a lady's head from olden days, with three little roses on one side of her hair, all curled and combed up, and above it, held up I don't know how, a big ship with rows of sails.

As soon as we were in the street, people started staring at us. I was dressed in black from head to toe and, to brighten it up a little, I'd stuck a red rose in my hair without asking his permission. Cosme's suit was pale yellow, with beige shoes, an olive green silk handkerchief in his breast pocket and on his vest a gold chain thick as the ones on wells. It had belonged to his great-great-grandfather. When we'd gotten on the trolley, a young guy with tousled hair said he'd like to fondle my rose. Cosme turned white with rage. As we climbed the stairs to the upper deck, the conductor peered at me from underneath. Luckily, Cosme went ahead. Just as I sat down by the aisle, since he'd taken my favorite spot by the railing, he tore the rose out of my hair and threw it over the side. The houses looked pretty going by and you could smell the magnolias. Cosme kept adding up how much what I was wearing had cost him, a terrifying sum. He said you could see none of my boyfriends had had the dough to dress me up right. And I was dumb enough to tell him how Eusebi and I had fallen in love when we were kids and about Andrés, who I'd never mentioned till then. Then he really started getting mad. Sitting on top of Tibidabo, with the ferris wheel turning, and later at a table sipping orxata with straws, he couldn't stop asking if I'd spent the night with those guys under the pine trees. To get my mind off all the nasty things he was saying, I watched the lights coming on and didn't answer him.

When we got into bed and he turned off the light, I couldn't sleep. The dress had run a little and stained my underarms, and, dying of heat, I'd climbed into the big sink to wash. Even there he kept bothering me. "How did you make a living?" he kept asking. "From those blouses? That's a lie!" And when he started snoring I felt like crying but I couldn't, because of his yelling and that ruined night and the rose he'd thrown away. The next day he tried to knock me out by throwing me down the stairs and I went tumbling down and fell on my backside. For two years, when the weather changed, the bottom bone of my spine would ache. I couldn't stand to be in that room for two hours straight. I couldn't bear that split lip and shiny gold tooth and those tiny hands. Everything made me sick: the dripping faucet, the lights on the ceiling, that woman who'd brought me milk the first day and whose face got longer by the week. And if I closed my eyes to keep from thinking I'd hear the faucet dripping and dripping and see the head on a baby boy who was killing his mother and afterward they sprinkled him with holy water and baptized him Cosme. When he'd come in, after going around laughing and chatting at all the tables, he'd look at me furiously and imitate my voice. "Andrés? Yes, right away. Eusebi? Yessir, coming right up." And all of a sudden his voice would get deeper and he'd shout "And let's have some more!" Finally I shouted back, even louder. "Let the dead rest in peace!" I yelled, leave the dead alone because one had died behind bars and the other bleeding and I started going out every afternoon because I couldn't stand it anymore. And I felt like working the Rambles again. To walk around at three in the morning and look at the clock on the opera house and touch that wall on Red Street and the iron gate outside the park. I'd sit down on benches and watch the cars go by. One day I told the horse-faced woman and she said if I sat there too long on that cold stone my womb would get chilled. Cosme never asked where I was going or where I'd been, no matter whether I came back early or late. But I always came back before ten. Till one Monday, which was the cook's day off, he was standing waiting for me by the bench with the lying-down statues. As soon as I saw him, I thought "Here we go." He told me, holding two fingers together very delicately, not to be alarmed, that he wanted to talk to me but not right there. And he took me to the Punyalada. He ordered two coffees and when the waiter had brought them he said very mysteriously that he had to talk about some delicate matters, since his children's bread was involved. He stretched out his left hand and showed me his wedding ring. He told me he had a son and a daughter who were the apples of his eye. The boy's health wasn't good. "I finish cooking and head straight for the drug store." And staring at me like he was trying to look deep inside me, he said I'd drive Cosme crazy and if he went crazy that'd be the end of his restaurant and with no restaurant he wouldn't be able to feed himself. "Whenever you leave," he said slowly, cupping his hand to one side of his mouth, "he's right behind you. He follows you around. They've seen him hiding behind a tree on the Rambla de Catalunya, devouring you with his eyes, and you sitting on a bench like a rose." He clasped his hands and begged me for the love of God to stay at home and stop wandering around the streets, and if I was bored to do something to amuse myself. "Why don't you sew? Cosme treats you like he's found a pearl in a mussel and can't get used to it and is scared you'll roll away. He's getting frantic."

⚘ **XXIV** I MANAGED TO PUT UP WITH IT FOR MORE than two years, and when I'd almost gotten used to it I started to get scared of getting used to it. One afternoon, with nothing but what I had on my back, I headed for Paulina's house. I hadn't seen her since that day with the hairpin. The garden was overgrown with weeds and the irises hadn't bloomed yet. For a moment I thought maybe she'd moved and there were other people living there. But no. The whole garden and the cypresses said Paulina. I wandered among the plants and sat down under a fig tree on a bench I hadn't seen the first time, but I got up pretty quick. Above, on the side with the white irises, there was a rosebush with buds. The spring air was chilly. I plucked a petal off a daisy, crushed it between my fingers, and sniffed that bitter smell that reminded me of rues and clover.

I saw her coming up the steps between the rows of cypresses, loaded down with packages, and as she came closer sometimes you could see her through the trees and sometimes you couldn't. She hadn't changed a bit. When she got to the door she put her packages down because she was panting, she looked at me awhile, we started laughing and she said to come in and she'd make me a cup of coffee. Inside it smelled like lavender and there was a vase of teasels. She started laughing again without taking her eyes off me and told me she was laughing because the night before a big holiday she'd seen me dressed up black and shiny like a seal, climbing onto the top deck of a trolley with a man who didn't look like my type.

I asked her how the gentleman from Tarragona was doing, and she said he was fine. Afterward, while we were having coffee, I told her what I'd been up to. She said she'd been lucky never to get involved with any jealous types, but it must be hell. She couldn't believe he'd followed me around the streets like a thief. "Jealous guys," she said, "are cheapskates, and they're always spying on you." I told her I didn't want to go back to the restaurant, how if I went back I'd be doomed forever, how one day he'd thrown me down the stairs, how just thinking about it made me sick, how I was fed up with cheap cooking oil and frying onions and garlic and myself and everything. She listened with a horrified look on her face, and when I'd finished she said we'd work it out. I could stay with her and tomorrow would be Saturday and the gentleman from Tarragona was coming and everything would straighten itself out. She spotted the glass heart and fell in love with it and I asked if she'd like it but she said no. I told her it was a keepsake from a day Andrés and I had gone for a stroll and I'd seen a very handsome navy officer and for her I wouldn't mind parting with it but it sort of kept me company.

I spent the night at Paulina's. The next day the gentleman from Tarragona came. I don't know how to describe him: he was part high-class and part peasant, with delicate hands from not working and lots of respect for the rain and sunshine. While we were having lunch, he said he and Paulina had discussed me and he'd introduce me to a very nice guy, the son of a friend of his who'd died years ago. The nice guy had a sickly wife, very delicate, and his two kids and the wife lived in the country with her parents. He said though his friend's son might not seem like it, he was a little on the wild side, not too well behaved, and he looked after his estates more for fun than work. His name was Marc. "I'm sure," he said, "that you'll like him, I mean you'll like each other. And he'll be thrilled to meet a girl with such sad eyes; yes, when you laugh they look even sadder. All you have to do is open your hand and cover the bottom of your face. Your mouth laughs, but not your eyes." And he even said I laughed without knowing why, like I was laughing for their sake. "Drink some more wine; it'll relax you."

While Paulina, dressed as a chambermaid, went to fix some coffee, the gentleman from Tarragona tapped my knee and said "I already told Paulina you can stay here as long as you need to."

୬ **XXV** MARC SHOWED UP TWO WEEKS LATER. WE'D just finished lunch and were sitting in front of the house. First you could hear his horn blowing while the gentleman from Tarragona was telling me how on the street with the bus stop they'd killed seven or eight people at the beginning of the revolution; and it blew for a good five minutes straight, like it was stuck. After it had stopped for a while, I saw a young man taking the steps two at a time. I thought he must be Marc, though Paulina and the gentleman from Tarragona hadn't said anything about expecting him. When he got there he looked at us, laughed, and bent over to tie a shoelace that had come untied while he was climbing. His hair fell forward and swayed a little. Then he sat down and the gentleman from Tarragona asked how he was getting along. I didn't move and just stared at him like a bird a snake is about to gobble up. All of a sudden the gentleman from Tarragona threw up his hands and asked us to excuse him for not introducing us. He added, laughing, that he'd noticed how we couldn't take our eyes off each other. I answered that I was looking at Marc because of his hair, which reminded me of a boy I'd known and who'd died. Marc shot me a dirty look, "Please don't talk like that," and changed the subject to the garden. How it seemed made especially for strolls on moonlit nights, down the paths and up the steps, long shadows, green gate, a little clearing, rocks and irises and more rocks and more irises. Paulina cut him short by saying the bad part was that at night the snails came out and took over the rocks and grass and every time you took a step you'd hear broken shells crunching and crunching.

Paulina brought out some fruit and Marc asked if we knew how to eat sliced bananas, cutting them up with a knife and fork on a plate. The gentleman from Tarragona said he was a very old-fashioned young man because you had to eat bananas like monkeys in palm trees. Marc wanted to know if there was a special breed of monkeys that lived in palm trees and we laughed and laughed in the sunshine with wisteria flowers fluttering down from time to time. Then we tried to see if we could cut slices the same size, faster and faster till there was nothing left to cut. While Paulina was making coffee, the gentleman from

Tarragona went to get the liqueurs and Marc asked where I'd gotten those eyes. And that laugh. But he didn't say any other nice things because before Paulina and the gentleman from Tarragona could come back he took my hand and led me away. We got in his car, which was a black convertible with a white hood, and just as we were sitting down he turned to me and said, I don't know if it was serious or a joke, that some really weird things happened in Barcelona. The wind blew my hair back and made my blouse flutter and I don't know where we went but after driving along dirt road after dirt road we were back in Barcelona. He did it three or four times. The bridges crossed rivers of sand cut by trickles of water, with shacks right down to the sand, glittering in the sunlight. You could see houses by themselves with gardens and flat roofs, pine groves on both sides of the road and an occasional cypress or railing around a balcony with pots of geraniums. We turned down a stretch of dirt road so bad the car bounced from hole to hole like a grasshopper. And smoke poured out of the chimneys. Finally he stopped and we went into a restaurant. The wind had drained all the blood from my face, I felt cold and looked like a beggar beside all those well-dressed people; but when Marc looked at me I felt like the best-dressed woman there. We ordered tea and he looked half-dazed, so moonstruck that I felt sorry for him, as if he couldn't believe I was really sitting there next to him, and then I suddenly felt this laughing fit coming on and bit my lip and my face got all red and he asked what was the matter and I couldn't answer because if I opened my mouth I'd have burst out laughing. I dug my nails into my palms to see if the pain would stop that urge to giggle that for some reason had come over me, and I remembered Cosme and saw his shadow behind a tree spying on me, and a big spider was sitting on top of the tree. And it was like I was dreaming till I realized I was staring at Marc's hand flat on the tablecloth with his fingers a little arched. I put my hand down, facing his so they were almost touching, and whispered "Tree and spider, tree and spider." And suddenly I couldn't hold it in any longer and laughed so hard everyone turned around to look at me.

When we were back in his car, Marc asked where I felt like going. I said the Rambla de Catalunya; I went all the way down it with my head thrown back, watching the patterns the lime tree leaves made. Then we drove all over again, criss-crossing the city, sometimes down crowded streets and sometimes down almost-deserted roads, swerving and blowing the horn for fun, and when it was pitch black we stopped at another restaurant beside a field where you could see strings of lights along the Diagonal. The doorman was wearing a red frock coat. Marc stopped the car and said instead of going right in it'd be nice to sit awhile in that field. When we were there he stuck his finger through one of my curls and said he'd been caught hook, line, and sinker. He started fluffing up my hair like he was crazy and whispering very calmly, "We'll make Cecília over, we'll dress her and undress her, we'll make her laugh and make her cry." He gripped my neck between his hands and kissed me on the lips and I got so angry that

I bit him and he slapped me. "So you won't do that again." And then he stuck his finger in the dimple on my cheek. "Gorgeous."

↝ **XXVI** MARC TAUGHT ME TO SMOKE. THE FIRST cigarette made me a little sick and left a bad taste in my mouth. But it was fun. With the cigarette in my lips, I waited for Marc to light it but he didn't. He absent-mindedly lit his own and handed me the lighter. I got used to smoking, and I liked to watch the smoke rings and swirls, and especially that burst of blue flame when you light a match. Marc rented half an apartment for me on Majorca Street. He said it was all he could find at the moment. For a few months I missed the house with the irises, with so much sky and those hills turning blue at sunset. Gradually I got over missing it. I spent hour after hour lying on an ottoman on the glassed-in porch with my back to the street, staring at a frieze on the dining room wall made of little angels and pomegranates sliced in half. Marc told me the apartment belonged to some rich people who lived in the country and came to Barcelona from time to time; they kept half of it for themselves because they didn't like hotels and rented the other half out. That's what he said and I believed him. In the foyer there was a little door, rather new, that was locked and led to the other half of the apartment. The first night, once Marc was gone, I stood in the foyer for a while looking at that door and feeling a little nervous.

Our apartment had a dining room and a bedroom that looked out on the street; the kitchen, the bathroom, and another smaller bedroom faced the airshaft. But as soon as I saw all that heavy black furniture and a wardrobe with a mirror so high it reached the ceiling, I decided to live and sleep on the porch as long as I was in that apartment, so I asked Marc to have the ottoman reupholstered in pearl gray and to get some cushions in all different colors so I wouldn't feel so gloomy. The day I went to look at the apartment I went by myself because Marc said he had work to do. It was on the third floor, and since I've always been scared of elevators, I decided to take the stairs. As soon as I started up, I saw a man peeking at my legs through a crack between the curtains in the concierge's lodge and I hugged the wall so he wouldn't see too much. The only thing I liked about that apartment was a hen. It looked like it was roosting on the sideboard, white with a crest like a red carnation falling over one eye. It was cut around the top, which you could lift off like the top of a box. I piled lots of pitchers and vases in a wardrobe in the little bedroom and at first, when Marc was coming, I'd sprinkle the bed with cologne to make it smell nice. I told him the truth, that I didn't care for that apartment. He said he didn't either but when two people get along nothing else matters and I should remember that place wasn't forever. The concierge came twice a week to do the heavy housework and I stayed to keep an eye on her. She always told the same story: how years ago she'd had an accident and hadn't been able to walk for months. She always told it exactly the same, about what the doctor had said and what she'd thought on nights when she couldn't sleep, not from the accident, which was dead and buried, but from worrying about never being able to walk again. I asked if she knew the people who lived next door; she shrugged her shoulders and chuckled. I'd never lived in an apartment and that street wasn't as pretty as the hills behind the house with the irises, but on rainy days I'd sit and watch the umbrellas go by. And I wished that whole street could be a sea of shiny umbrellas in all colors, with no people or cars, just umbrellas with thunder and lightning overhead.

One night I thought a burglar had broken in. It must have been around midnight. I went out in the hall and tiptoed into the foyer. You couldn't hear a thing. I got scared and pushed a chair against the door with its back below the lock so no one could sneak in. The doorbell woke me late the next morning; it kept ringing like crazy. I went to open it and saw Marc, who'd never come at that time of day. He told me he didn't like jokes and if I ever blocked the door again it was all over between us.

Some days Marc attracted me and I felt like I was in love with him and thought maybe we could get married if his wife would only die. But other days he made me jumpy and I stared at him when he wasn't looking and wondering what was going through his head, whether it was good or bad. As long as I was in the house with the irises he'd taken me for rides, but that had barely lasted two months and once I was in the apartment we stopped going out. Sometimes he wouldn't show up for a week and when he finally did he'd say he'd been with his family. He told me proudly and happily, like he was trying to make me jealous, and I'd rather not have known where he'd been.

XXVII MY NEXT DOOR NEIGHBOR WAS NAMED Constància. Whenever I went out or came home, her front door was open. I thought she was one of those people who couldn't stand living behind closed doors. The first time we said hello was one morning when I was about to go down the stairs and she was coming out of the elevator dressed in black and wearing a hat with artificial violets on it. She was tall and fat. From the back, with her swollen legs and ankles, she looked like an elephant. All she needed was a tail.

One day when I was feeling affectionate I told Marc I was pregnant and he said he'd disown the child. I didn't get mad, because it was something to make you sad, not mad. But it cleared my head a little and I stopped being so crazy about him. That's why the day Senyora Constància invited me to see the clock in her apartment, I was happy to accept. It was on the mantle above the fireplace in her dining room, which was right next to mine. It was gilded, and above the round clockface there were two towers like on a castle. Each tower had a balcony all around the top. Since it was a few minutes before the hour, we sat down on her porch and she told me about her health. Just when I was starting to get bored, a very delicate little bell chimed and then another louder one right after it. We got up and went back in the dining room to see the clock. The doors on the balconies had opened and two little black-and-gold figurines had come out. One was a girl holding out her left hand. The other was a soldier raising his right hand with a red enameled flower in it. The figurines moved round and round as long as the bells kept chiming and it seemed like the soldier wanted to give the flower to the girl, who wanted to take it. But they always passed each other without touching and when the bells stopped chiming they entered their little doors, turned around so they were facing outward, and the doors shut. Through some bars like in a jail you could see them standing there till the bell rang again and the doors opened. As I was on my way out, Senyora Constància took me into the kitchen and showed me a fish she'd bought; the smell was so strong I thought I'd puke and wondered if what I'd told Marc as a joke could be true. When I was back in my apartment, I got sick again thinking about that fish and Senyora Constància's knees because she'd showed them to me, hiking her skirts halfway up her thighs, all covered with lumps, and she'd told me her circulation was bad, that the doctors stuck needles a foot long in her knees to empty them. All the time she kept touching the broken strap on a slip that was lying neatly folded on the coffee table on her porch. When we were at the door she showed me a wart on one side of her tongue that made her salivate while she was talking.

I had to run into the bathroom and when Marc came I told him there were three of us now. He didn't reply. He came back the next day, took out his wallet, and gave me some money to get rid of it. I didn't have to because I had a miscarriage, too early to know what I'd had. Between Marc and me, or more exactly between me and Marc, something snapped; and I heard the sound. Like a very skillful hand had torn a silk dress. Rip.

❧ **XXVIII** I FELT PRETTY WEAK AND THE DOCTOR SAID I should sunbathe and eat lots of red meat. I went down the stairs very slowly because my belly felt heavy, but the one time I tried taking the elevator I felt like my insides had gone topsy-turvy and I was about to scream. I walked around for a while looking in store windows and then sat down on a bench and began chain-smoking. One day when I was cold and felt worn out, I went into a café to have something to drink. It was a café I'd discovered a few days earlier but I hadn't gone in yet, even though I liked it because to get in you had to climb a few steps and it had a revolving door. I enjoyed being there so much that I started going every day. I'd choose a seat near the window and stay for a long time looking out at the plane trees and the people and cars going by. After two or three weeks, just as I was raising my cup to my lips, the waiter, who knew me from seeing me so often, came up and said there was a gentleman who was very eager to speak with me. I turned a little and spotted him right away. He was an old man, thin, with white hair and a little pointy beard. He was sitting very straight at a table in the back, facing the light. The waiter asked what I wanted him to say, whether the gentle-

man should come to me or would I go to him. Since he was
so old I said I'd go to him. The waiter picked up my cup
and took it to the gentleman's table, and I, very politely because he seemed so respectable, asked what he wanted.
First he asked if I'd be kind enough to sit down. He told
me he'd been a general and owned two castles on both
sides of a river that was his too, not very wide of course,
and in that stretch of river, which was full of trout, no one
could fish but him.

He went on talking in a cracked voice that every so often
would get clear. He told me he was well off and then out of
the blue he asked if I liked botany. I said when I was little
I'd studied anatomy but I couldn't remember a thing about
it. He asked if I'd like another coffee and I said no because
I wouldn't be able to sleep that night. As soon as I'd said it
I realized that I should have thought of another reason because it was barely mid-morning, but he kept on talking as
if he hadn't even heard me. He said he felt lonely, that his
two nephews had abandoned him, that one was nuts and
the other close to it, and they got it from him. That he'd
give anything to have a little youth around him, that it
would prolong his life and be a good deed because, he said
very naturally, "If I die, where do dead people's souls go?"
He turned to face me, put his hands flat on the table, and
said his soul attracted dead spirits. He added that as soon
as he got up he read the funeral notices, dressed as quickly
as he could, and attended as many burials as he could get
to, people he didn't know, it made no difference. He'd
stand at the back, dressed in mourning, and as soon as the

crowd entered the cemetery the dead soul would join with his. Then he asked if I'd like to see his apartment, but right away. And since I had nothing to do and wasn't expecting Marc till that evening, I said that since he insisted. . . . And because I was bored, and because I'd liked all that stuff about dead souls.

He lived a couple of blocks away. It was a fancy building, with one staircase to the other apartments and another just for his, which was on the second floor. The banister of his staircase was made of chiseled stone like embroidery and in the middle of the courtyard there was a fountain with water shooting up in the air. Halfway up the stairs he had to stop because he was gasping, and when he could open his mouth to speak he said he suffered from asthma. He stuck his key in the lock but before he could turn it the door opened and we saw a servant with a face like a peasant's and a gray-and-black-striped vest. The old man showed me into a very big room full of furniture and shadows even though it had three balconies. In front of the center balcony there was a cage on a column and in one corner a grand piano. I went over to look in the cage, and the old man told me it was empty, that he'd had some canaries but they'd sung so much he'd gotten sick of hearing them and opened the door. They'd all flown away, one after the other. Then he had me sit down in an easy chair with a purple silk cushion on one arm; when he saw me looking at it he asked if I liked purple. Before I could answer, he left and came back in different clothes.

He asked me to stay to lunch. The servant set a round

table with a lace tablecloth, plates with gold edges, and goblets with red bottoms, and in the middle of the table he put a silver vase full of white and yellow roses. Meanwhile I looked at the tapestry on the wall at the other end, full of soldiers and lances. In the middle there was a horse rearing up, with a checkered pennant fluttering on its head and the checks got smaller and smaller the closer you got to the tip. On the ground in a clump of gray, there was a stone that looked like an egg in a nest.

The lunch began with a clear soup that tasted like julienne and when we'd finished it the servant brought a long, narrow platter shaped like a fish, and inside there was a fish covered with gelatin. We ate it all. The old man said it had been caught in a river, but you could see from a mile away that it hadn't been, and when the servant had shown him the platter before setting it down, he'd whistled under his breath and said "What a fish!" For dessert we had all kinds of cheese and finally, when nothing was left, the old man got up, went to the end of the room and stopped in front of a high, narrow cabinet beside the tapestry, full of little drawers. He hunted around for a while and then came back and gave me a rolled wafer. I ate it very slowly because the crunching made me self-conscious since I was the only one eating it. He asked if it was good and I said yes. Then he went out, came back with a big book, sat down, made me move my chair so it was right next to his, opened the book where he wanted to, stuck his finger on a flower and said "See? That's mustard."

⚇ **XXIX** JUST AS I OPENED THE DOOR I HEARD THE phone and when I reached it, it stopped ringing. I lay down on the ottoman, thinking that compared to the air in that general's apartment, the air in the street smelled fresh and sweet as a rose, and a half hour later, while I was dozing, the phone rang again. I picked it up, said "Hello," and the voice at the other end said "Sorry. Wrong number." As I was dozing off again, I thought happily about how I was going to buy a pink dress.

When Marc came at ten, I was asleep. Without giving me time to figure out where I was, I'd been sleeping so soundly, he asked me where I'd been. I told him I'd gone out for a walk. He didn't reply, but after a while he piped up again and said he didn't like being fooled with and as tired as I'd been since I'd left the clinic, I'd be better off not going out so much. I just sat there, because it seemed like he was trying to make me mad, and when he asked if I'd done anything else, I said no. And the truth was I felt so groggy I didn't even remember that gentleman with the castles. He said why didn't I find some girlfriend to go out with and keep me company. I said sometimes I visited the lady next door but I didn't like her because she had a wart on her tongue and showed me her thighs. Then he said he was going away for three months and, since I'd been getting more and more annoyed, I answered that I wasn't surprised and maybe sometime he'd find a couple of hours to spend with me. In a slightly cold voice, he said I couldn't need him that much with all the time I wasted going to cafés and other places. I hit him in the chest, he sat there stiff as a board, and I shouted that I wasn't going to hang around the house all day knitting and asking his permission to get a little fresh air. He didn't touch me, but the dirty look he shot me was enough. When he was gone I thought I'd made a mistake and maybe I should have told him I'd had lunch with that general. I went out on the porch and sat there for a long time, wide awake . . . until the sun rose.

Before nine they called again and when I asked who it was the voice said sorry, wrong number. I stayed home all that day. The next morning when I opened the door, I saw my next door neighbor on the landing, wearing her hat with those violets and she muttered something about going to buy plastic flowers for a pot. As we were going down the stairs I asked if anyone had ever called her and then said right away it was a wrong number. She answered so fast I couldn't understand a word she said. To avoid the general, I kept away from that café for seven or eight days and instead of walking toward the Passeig de Gràcia I went toward the Diagonal. I was very bored. One morning I saw a wedding at the Pompeia Church and stopped to wait for the bride and groom to come out. As they were having their picture taken I caught a glimpse of the bride through the crowd, all dressed in pretty white lace from head to toe, with a cloud of tulle that started at her shoulders and went to her pointy silver shoes. They took one shot of them gazing into each other's eyes, and they looked so lovesick I had to turn away to keep from puking. I went back the way I'd come, and since I didn't know where to go and didn't feel like walking around, I wandered into the café with the general. He was sitting at his usual table and you could see he'd been waiting for me because as soon as I came in he waved to me to come over. He asked where I'd been hiding since he hadn't seen me in so long and then invited me to please have supper with him that evening, and how he'd gotten a book with leaves pasted in it down from the top of a bookshelf and he'd tell me about how mandrakes scream.

That afternoon I went shopping for a pink dress. I'd forgotten all about it. The ones I saw weren't quite what I had in mind, some because the pink was too bright and others because it was too pale, but what annoyed me was that one I liked all right, though I wasn't crazy about it, was tight and the salesgirl tried to persuade me to take it, saying that was the style. Though I really didn't feel like it, I went to the general's house for supper. The servant with the striped vest let me in. He set the table, and the julienne soup, the platter with the fish in gelatin, and the cheeses appeared: all the same. Then, like the first day, the old man spent a long time in front of the cabinet with the little drawers hunting for a wafer. When I'd eaten it, we sat down by the cage and he started telling me weird stories about plants. I arrived home exhausted and a moment later the phone rang. I picked it up, resigned, and as usual a voice said "Sorry." And not a word from Marc.

I spaced out my visits to Senyora Constància, but one day, fingering the broken strap on that slip she always kept folded on the coffee table, she said men were like babies, poor guys. . . . And then I don't know what happened but I started to hate her. And every day it got worse. She must have noticed, and especially that I was avoiding her, and maybe that's why she started pestering me. She was always underfoot. Once when I went to buy some aspirin at the drug store, the clerk said every time I went there she'd drop by a moment later and ask what I'd bought. Till one day I ran into her in the grocery store, she pulled me aside, and very mysteriously, with her lips almost touching my cheek, she whispered that they were spying on me from the building across the street.

◦ **XXX** THE NEXT DAY I MET HER ON THE LANDING, talking to a short, fat man with a round face pink as a crayfish. She introduced us. He was her younger brother. All three of us started laughing, me because it seemed so weird that a guy like that would be such a big lady's brother and them without knowing why I was laughing and just to be polite. Two weeks later she introduced me to another brother, older than her, whose face was also pink, but he was taller than the first one. No matter how hard I tried, I couldn't avoid her. I oiled the lock and, to fool her, I'd open the door a few times like I was going out and then sneak back inside to see if I could wear her out. But when I got back, no matter what time it was, she was always waiting on the landing. She must have lived with her eye glued to the peephole, looking and listening. One day she wasn't on the landing and I thought maybe she'd died. That was the day the shenanigans with the doormat started. As I was putting the key in the lock, it seemed like something had changed. It was the doormat, which was crooked, with one corner up against the door. I absent-mindedly straightened it with my foot, happy to be able to come home in peace. The next day the same thing happened: the doormat, which must have been in its normal place when I went out because I hadn't even noticed it, was turned around again with the short end facing the other side of the landing. I don't know how many days this stunt lasted. She'd come out when I was away, kick the doormat so it was crooked, and duck back inside. It must have been her way of telling me she knew I'd gone out. The worst part was I couldn't say anything because I never caught her in the act. One morning I made it crooked myself and went out doubled over with laughter. At midday, when I came back, it was in its usual place. I kicked it again and the next day it was straight. And meanwhile the phone would ring every day. They'd stopped saying "Sorry, wrong number" and would ask if there were any tickets left for the afternoon show or whether Senyora Maspons or Senyor Martí was around. I said no, no, no, very patiently, and lots of days I'd leave the phone off the hook for hours. The concierge came and went, and her husband peeked at my legs whenever he could. I didn't hear a peep out of Marc for days and the general invited me to supper a couple of times a week. I didn't like seeing him but I went anyway because I felt funny staying at home.

One day when he'd invited me I met Senyora Constància's brothers on the landing. They were carrying some big packages tied with string and had left the elevator door open. I was about to walk by but they said hello and one asked me to please step inside. And I still don't know how it happened but I found myself in the elevator with those two brothers, and the younger one said they might as well enjoy it and the older one put down his packages and tried to undo the top button on my blouse. I stamped on his toe so hard he screamed and when we stepped out of the elevator I saw he was limping. They hadn't done anything, but my blood was boiling. I entered the general's apartment like it was Heaven and while I was waiting in his huge sitting room, I went up to the tapestry to look at that stone in the nest and I touched it. That day he said I'd never told him anything about my life, and he asked what I did, if I had a family or boyfriend. After supper, when he went to fetch the wafer, he stood there like he was frozen in front of the cabinet with the little drawers. It seemed like he wanted to move but couldn't. I didn't know what to do and maybe because he was so still he reminded me of the man with no skin in Senyor Jaume's tower, and then I saw him changed into a tree of nerves with his brain on top like a splotch of milk and the tail on his brain draining down through his spine. The servant led him away, and I got out as fast as I could. When I got home, I had to run to the bathroom and throw up the whole meal.

Marc showed up the next morning, without calling first, and instead of being happy to see him I told him to look for another apartment, that the one I was in was getting on my nerves. He ran his fingers through my hair, laughing, and

said he was working on it but it was hard because he
wanted to find someplace really nice. I got the feeling he
was just saying it to shut me up, and I was about to tell him
what Senyora Constància did, but I thought he'd be capa-
ble of telling me I was nuts. He left very quickly saying he
had work to do and when he was on the landing he said
he'd come more often. I dressed and went out. Since I felt
like seeing new faces I went into a café on the Diagonal
where I'd never been before. Above the banquettes, in
some lit-up glass cases, there were pressed ferns that
made patterns like fine brocade. I enjoyed that café because it seemed like I could hide away there and I'd stick
out less because it was so small. And since Marc's return
had been more of a pain than anything else, I started going
there a lot. I always saw the same faces and I liked thinking how the other sides of those ferns in the glass were
covered with little furry chocolate-colored spots. Soon I
noticed some men who were sitting down when I came in
and were still there when I left. They sat in the back and I
got used to sitting there too. One of them wore a suit with
tiny checks, silk socks with little holes in them, and low
tan shoes, so shiny you could see your face in them. Since
they were always deep in conversation, I looked at them
the whole time and imagined I was a little sick girl and
they'd come to visit me and keep me company. The man
with the checked suit's shoes had a pattern of little holes
on the toes and around the heels. Sometimes he'd cross his
legs and swing one of them back and forth and the shoe
would come and go, flashing as it moved. Some days I'd

feel an urge to hug him, to stick my hands in all his pockets and unbutton his vest. When I got tired of looking at
his shoe, I'd look at his ear. It wasn't like a murderer's; the
lobe was round and stood out from his head. The gentleman who sat facing me was fat and I didn't like him much
because he had a cheerful look on his face. He was very
well dressed too. One day I realized he'd caught me staring
at the man with the shoes. And I felt embarrassed.

XXXI I'D NEVER BEEN ABLE TO WEAR A BRA BE-
cause my breasts were so small that when I raised my arm,
even if the bra was very tight, it would ride up around my
neck. But I had to do something if I was going to wear that
pink dress I'd finally bought and which was so tight you
could see everything. I'd spent all night looking at myself
in the mirror, sometimes thinking I looked okay and sometimes that I looked indecent. I went in lots of shops and
department stores, searching for a nice bra but with no
luck till I discovered a little shop where everything seemed
pretty and well made. The lady who ran it told me not to
get a separate bra and girdle and said I'd feel more secure
in a corset. Because of the way I was built, I couldn't wear
a bra.

She showed me lots of corsets: pink, black, and white
ones. With elastic on the sides so you could move around
inside them. Some with backs and others backless so you
could wear low-cut gowns. Some had straight straps and
others had crossed ones. With rubber clasps hidden by lit-

tle silk bows. She showed me one made of turquoise satin covered with lace, with a lace ruffle on the bottom that must have been a nuisance but couldn't have been prettier. I fell in love with it. Since the fancy ones cost much more than I could afford, she brought out some others made of patterned elastic, with openwork like they'd been sewn and a design made of leaves and branches, and down the middle there was a strip of satin with a zipper. I bought one of those. I complained that it was a little tight, but she said it should be like that, that after I'd worn it awhile it would give, that I'd get used to it in a jiffy and not even realize I was wearing it. And she said it gave me a great figure. On the dressing room walls there were some little engravings of old-fashioned ladies in corsets. One showed a lady with lots of hair and red-and-white-striped stockings, with bloomers down to below her knees and flared at the bottom and a corset that pushed her breasts up so high they looked like they were on a tray. A chambermaid with a coif was lacing up the corset, with her knee against the lady's back for more leverage. The lady was wearing high shoes with dark, round buttons like partridge eyes.

Since the lady who owned the shop had advised me to wear the corset around the house so I'd get used to it and it would stretch, as soon as I got home I hurried to put it on. I looked at myself in the mirror, and I felt like a real vamp. I had a bunch of little blue ribbony roses on my bosom, surrounded by pale green moss. I left it on to sleep and got into bed thinking soon I'd be able to wear the pink dress. I'd already bought some pink shoes and a necklace with pink beads, big ones all the same size, the kind that fit tight around your neck like a dog's collar, a cheap doll's necklace that had cost next to nothing.

I woke up feeling like I was wearing a suit of armor. My body ached and I'd dreamt I was suffocating tied up in a sack. The corset had been squeezing me and I had to take it off like I was tearing off my skin because the zipper was stuck. When I ran my hands along my sides to soothe them, the skin felt so bumpy that I looked in the mirror. You could see the pattern from the elastic leaves and branches on my skin. It didn't disappear till the next day.

When I went out shopping that morning, I got a surprise. Senyora Constància, who hadn't been on the landing since she'd started fooling with my doormat, was waiting for me, stiff as a broom. She asked why I never visited her, she invited me to come in, and she said, very oozy and chummy, that she thought about me all the time, that if I wanted she could introduce me to one of her nephews or, if I preferred, a banker friend of hers, a real gentleman, elderly, because she said, "A girl in your profession should make the most of her charms." She sighed and explained that her husband had left her for a fortune teller and she'd had to do all kinds of jobs to make a living. I just stared at her and thought, "God, you're ugly!" because all I cared about was that pink dress and the pink necklace to attract that handsome gentleman in the café with the ferns who'd never even looked at me. And I bought a bottle of sexy cologne.

ॐ **XXXII** CAREFULLY BATHED, COMBED, AND DRESSED,
with a dab of perfume behind each ear and my nails like
ten tiny mirrors, I sat down on a chair in the dining room to
straighten out my purse. The next thing I knew my breasts
were as high as that lady's in the engraving. I paced around
the dining room a few times, worrying, and finally decided
to take off the corset and go as I was. The streets looked
pretty and it was like the sky had just been washed. I didn't
even remember that, while I was undressing to take off the
corset, the phone had rung twice and I'd ignored it. There
was a sports car parked in front of the Pompeia Restaurant. Two young guys were leaning against the car, one in a
light blue sweater and the other in a dark blue one with a
red kerchief around his neck. As I passed, the one in the
light blue sweater, who was facing me and must have seen
me coming, said, "Did you ever see a dream walking?" I
kept on like I hadn't noticed, and one of them whistled.
Some things are hard to explain: those two guys, who another day might have cheered me up, threw a kind of
shadow over my happiness at wearing that new outfit.
Who knows why? In the café, the waiter, who was young
and new on the job, touched my shoulder and said he'd
asked me three times what I wanted and I hadn't answered. It must have been true; I don't know. All I know is
I felt devastated because I'd hoped to make an entrance,
what they call a grand entrance, in the pink dress, and it
turned out that none of those gentlemen was there. When
the waiter put the cup down on the table he leaned over a
little more than he had to and whispered in my ear, "Roses

are red . . ." I drank my first sip of coffee without even looking at him.

They didn't stay away long. I saw their silhouettes before they came in and didn't stop looking at them out of the corner of my eye till they were sitting at their table. The handsome guy, who as usual sat with his back half to me, smoothed his hair and then I noticed his watch. The face was black and the numbers glittered whenever the light caught them. Instead of a strap, it had a gold band as thick as two fingers. I was getting bored and wondering what the hell I was doing there between the table and the glass case with those men talking and laughing without even noticing me, dressed in pink like a jerk and with my feet tucked under the table so they wouldn't see my shoes. I wanted to get away but I didn't dare; I was sure they'd see my thighs outlined against the light, and I kept wondering what to do till they left. In the street, I felt naked. I thought how the phone had rung twice, how I'd find the doormat crooked, and I started feeling jumpy. All of a sudden I felt like I was being followed. I could feel it in my skin. They must have started following me when I was still on the Diagonal and maybe they'd waited for me, hiding behind a palm tree. I didn't dare turn around because I didn't want the people following me to realize I was onto them. When I reached my building, I turned around and there was no one there. The concierge's husband ogled my legs as usual, and as soon as I got home I took off the pink dress and never put it on again with my own hands. I was sure I was being watched, that I was surrounded by eyes I couldn't see. I opened the curtains and looked in all the corners. It would be hours before Marc came and I didn't know what to do; I paced to and fro, I stood awhile staring out at the landing through the peephole, and I lay down on the ottoman to see if I could sleep. The phone woke me. I picked it up and a man's voice said he had to see me. I said there was nothing he had to see me about and he said yes, there was, it was very important, and I said I wasn't used to seeing people whose names I didn't know and I asked what his name was. He wouldn't say; he just repeated that he had to talk to me, and he insisted so much that finally, so he wouldn't think I was a namby-pamby afraid of having a drink, since he'd asked me to come out and have a drink, I said I'd wait for him in the lobby. I don't know why, but I asked if he lived in the neighborhood. He said yes, and as I hung up I could hear him laughing.

I saw him coming, with his chest out like he was trying to make himself look taller, because he was short. He had a loaf of bread under one arm. There were two big bald patches on his forehead, and everything about him breathed a kind of uneasiness, and a self-satisfaction that got on my nerves. We went into the first café we saw, and then I noticed his lips. I'd never seen anything like them; they were weird-looking, and the upper one was puckered and wavy like a chain of flowers. We talked about the weather, whether I liked to read, what I did. I told him I was very busy and he chortled a little. After a half hour chatting about nothing in particular, he said he had to get back to work, he paid, and we left. In the lobby I held my hand out so he'd realize it was time to go, but he wouldn't take it; he said he'd walk me to the elevator. When we were at the door I said I never used it, that I took the stairs, and I held out my hand again but he opened the door, pushed me a little, and when the elevator started he gripped my arm and shoved me into a corner so I could hardly move. He tried to kiss me and I turned away as much as I could and he searched for my lips and when he was about to find them I sucked them in and bit them. He followed me out of the elevator and as I was putting the key in the lock, he begged me to let him in. I didn't want to get mad because I still couldn't figure out what was happening and, laughing, I told him to go eat his loaf of bread, to beat it, and he stood there beside me, stubborn and surprised, and even then he asked me two more times to let him in. I pushed him away, he grabbed my hand and squeezed it to hurt me and with his eyes bugging out of his head he whispered furiously that I'd be sorry. I shut the door, so upset that I tripped and fell, spilling all the water on the floor, because there was a bucket in the foyer full of dirty water. Late that night, even though I'd gone right away to tell the concierge's husband she'd left her bucket in my apartment and should come and get it, that bucket was still in the foyer.

◈ **XXXIII** I COULDN'T GET TO SLEEP, THINKING about that bucket. I got up and went to see if they'd taken it away at the last minute without telling me, but the bucket was still there, with the mop lying on the floor. Just as I was reaching for the mop, I saw something little and gray sticking out under the door that led to the other half-apartment. I bent down to look: it was a bit of cloth. It was so tiny that I couldn't grab it, but I got scared because I thought it was sticking out a little less than before I'd bent down, as if they'd pulled it back. I thought a little scrap of cloth shouldn't scare me and tried to pull it toward me with my nail. I couldn't. I went to get a needle, stuck it in the cloth, and while I was trying to edge it toward me they gave a yank from the other side and it disappeared. I ran down the hall and shut myself in the bedroom. My heart was pounding. When I'd calmed down I went back to the foyer. The keyhole in the door to the other half-apartment was bright, like a light was shining on the other side. I tiptoed over, bent down, and when my eye was against the keyhole it went dark like there was another eye on the other side. I turned off the light and kept still, hardly breathing. After a long time, since I couldn't hear a thing, I opened the front door and left the mop and bucket on the landing.

I didn't get to sleep till just after daybreak. I woke up a few hours later with a headache, and the first thing I did was go out on the landing to see if they'd taken away the bucket. I ran back in the bedroom and slept till it was time to go to the café with the ferns. To me it was like water in a desert. I wore normal clothes and all the men were there except him. But I, because I needed him, knew he'd come and that, even though he always sat half-facing away, he'd noticed me. I didn't take my eyes off the door, and soon I saw his silhouette. He walked in front of me, he was wearing a very light gray suit, and as soon he reached his table he turned the collar on his jacket up and rubbed his hands together like he was freezing, even though it was warm, and then he looked at me with his eyes bright and laughing like a kid's and sat down facing me. I pretended to pick something up off the floor so he wouldn't think I was paying any attention to him. And everything stopped: the fear and anxiety. Even though I didn't look at him. I looked at his shoes. And that day one of his friends who was sitting at a table further away with a man I didn't recognize, talking in whispers like they were discussing business, stuck out his foot when I left and if I hadn't stepped aside he would have tripped me. I got back to my apartment laughing and thinking how he'd tried to trip me, and when I reached the dining room I felt like something had changed. It was hard to figure out what it was, because everything looked the same. It was the hen. I'd always kept it facing the porch, and now it was turned around with its tail where its head should be and its head facing the other way. It couldn't have been the concierge because it wasn't her day to clean. I stood there for a while staring at it, as if the white china could tell me what had happened, but I was still feeling too good and lay down on the ottoman with my face buried in the cushions and started thinking about the watch and ring on that man at the café with the ferns, a big ring with his initials and his wedding ring underneath it. That wedding ring annoyed me and I wished I hadn't seen it, as if wedding rings were a hideous deformity on men's ring fingers.

That evening Marc came and stared at me the whole time like he was staring at something really strange. I told him I didn't want the concierge to have a key to the apartment, that I'd clean it, that I didn't want the concierge in my house, and I pounded my fists against his chest, and he gripped my arms and said he'd ask her for the key, and he kept asking me what was the matter and every time he asked I said nothing was the matter, that I wanted the concierge's key. He went to ask for it and gave it to me. I hugged him happily, though I felt more like crying. He said he was in a very bad mood, he'd been trying not to show it but that business with the key had made it even worse and he asked me to stop going to that café every morning. I froze. I didn't know what to say or do, I went out on the porch, came back in the dining room and said there was no harm in me going to a café. He glared at me and I asked who'd told him I went to a café. He said that had nothing to do with it. I told him furiously that neither he nor anyone else was going to stop me from going to a café. He buttoned up his jacket, said we'd see about that, and left.

That night the knocking started. At first I couldn't figure out where it was coming from but then I realized it was the wall with the fireplace. Senyora Constància must have felt like playing. They were muffled knocks, like someone was using a hammer wrapped in a blanket, four in a row, then silence, and when it seemed like they'd stopped they started up again. I couldn't fall asleep and got up a few times to see if there was light coming through the door to the other half-apartment. The next day I arrived exhausted at the café with the ferns and realized the only things that kept me going were that café and the gentleman who sat facing me.

๑ **XXXIV** FOR A FEW DAYS, MAYBE A WEEK, NOTHING new happened. Some nights, not all of them, I heard knocks above the fireplace and every day when I got home I'd find the doormat different from how I'd left it. Three or four times, at night, I felt like someone was in the hall or the kitchen. The first time I stayed in bed, scared out of my wits. The others I tiptoed up to the dining room door, held my breath and listened awhile, and suddenly pushed it open, shaking from head to toe. I never saw anyone and only one time, the second, it seemed like a chair was out of place. I didn't close my eyes all night, thinking and listening, and since I couldn't give up going to that café with the ferns every morning, I spent almost all my afternoons sleeping. The weather didn't help; it was cloudy, the days were getting shorter and the wind slowly stripped the leaves off trees.

One afternoon when I was sitting on the porch, not thinking or looking at anything, because some afternoons I felt like they'd drained me out little by little, I suddenly noticed that on a glassed-in porch on the building across the street someone was waving to me. It was the man with the puckered lip. I felt like I'd seen some nasty wild beast, but I turned away like I hadn't spotted him, and a minute later he shot back inside. He was a tailor. I knew a tailor lived across the street, because I'd noticed that on the porch across from mine there was a dummy with gray hair and a frock coat. But I'd never noticed the people in the apartment.

Marc showed up earlier than usual with a friend I'd never seen. I gave them some cognac and had a sip myself, because a little cognac made me chatty but too much went straight to my head. Since all three of us smoked, the dining room quickly got cloudy. Marc's friend had pale blond hair and a black silk patch over one eye. His name was Eladi. And Marc, when he introduced us, said he was an historian. The eye without the patch was blue as a flower. To greet me he took one of my hands between his and, staring into my eyes with that flower-eye of his, he kissed my hand with his lips barely touching it. Marc said he'd be away again for a couple of months and had asked Eladi to keep me company.

As soon as they were gone, I pulled down the blinds and turned off the dining room light. Right away I spotted the tailor, who was staring at my porch. He must have had a grand old time seeing me dressed any old way, especially in the morning or when I got up at night because in the summer I'd sleep naked or in filmy, transparent nightgowns. Suddenly he turned around. His wife was coming from the back of the apartment and when she reached the porch, he began brushing off the dummy. He went a little further inside and, since his wife had her back to him and couldn't see what he was doing, from time to time he glanced at my porch like he couldn't keep his eyes off it. His wife's skin was reddish. She was skinny and walked with her head and shoulders jutting forward and her belly so far in that in profile she looked like a bow for shooting arrows. When she left, he went out on the porch again and just stood there staring. Maybe he couldn't grasp that the blinds were down. I couldn't sleep that night. I wasn't used to sleeping in the dark and I felt like I was smothering. But I covered my head, feeling like the tailor could see me through the blinds. As soon as I got up I went to peek through the slats and to my amazement I saw Senyora Constància giving an envelope to the doorman outside the building across the street who was sweeping the entrance. I went to the café with the ferns, almost passing out from tiredness, but first I brought the doormat inside so that lady couldn't have any more fun with it.

From that day on, whenever I got home I'd run to the blinds and always see the tailor staring, because he must have seen me go in and know I was peeking at him; they must have been trying to scare me. He even looked my way while he was fitting suits and one day I laughed to myself because I thought how he must be messing them up. That was the day I noticed a coffee-colored car half a block long parked on the other side of the street. And that day with the car I found the first photo.

꿈 **XXXV** THE PHOTO WAS OF MARC AND A LADY WHO must have been his wife. They were in a garden, sitting on a bench; she had a cigarette between her lips and he, leaning over, was offering her a light. Behind them were some flowers that looked like hydrangeas, but the photo was a little blurry and you couldn't tell for sure. On the right was a big round thing like a slice of watermelon. I found the picture on the floor under the bathroom sink, and I left it there. But now and then I'd go and look at it. I'd pick it up, hold it for a while, and put it back on the floor. To see the expression on Marc's face when he was with his wife, an expression I'd never seen, full of respect and devotion. She wasn't pretty. She was wearing a summer dress, open at the top, and a fine gold chain around her neck with a medallion tucked under the dress. Her hair was neatly combed back and gathered; you could see it was fine and there was a lot of it. After looking at the picture four or five times, I spotted her wedding ring; it had a big diamond on it.

I lived in the dark so the tailor wouldn't see me and sometimes, when I had to be in the bedroom for a while, I'd put a chair in front of the balcony with a pile of clothes over the back. One morning through the blinds I spotted the tailor's wife, very still, staring at my porch, which I'd never seen her do before. Down below that coffee-colored car was parked, and after keeping my eye on it for a while, because I wanted to find out whose it was, I heard the clock with the towers chiming like it was right inside my apartment. It gave me a start. I ran inside thinking they must have drilled a hole from Senyora Constància's dining room and I started poking the wall to see if the paper would give. I couldn't find a thing. I went in the kitchen to

look for the wire I used to unclog the sink and began poking under the moldings to see if they'd made it above the
floor tiles. I walked to the café without seeing anything,
like the streets and buildings didn't exist. All I saw was
that photo with the hydrangeas, and all I heard was that
hammer knocking against the wall.

But then I had a few days' rest. For the moment, that tailor disappeared off his porch and the phone stopped ringing. I still spent a couple of nights listening for sounds in
the foyer and waiting for those knocks, but since I couldn't
hear anything I started to relax. The photo had disappeared. One afternoon I'd left it under the bathroom sink
when I'd finished looking at it, and the next day it was
gone. Maybe Marc, who the day he'd introduced me to
Eladi had said he'd be gone for a while but didn't actually
get around to leaving, had picked it up and taken it away.
With the doormat in the apartment, I didn't spend so
much time wondering how it would look when I got back.
And since after all there was no way to figure out how from
the porch I'd been able to hear the chimes on Senyora
Constància's clock, I started thinking maybe I'd dreamt it.
I only thought that for a few days, because all that peace
and quiet went up in smoke as quickly as it had started.
One morning I found another photo in the drawer on the
night table in the bedroom, where I only slept when Marc
was there. You could see a deserted beach, and in the water two boys' heads were bobbing. In the middle of the
sand, wearing a funny-looking hat, was Marc's wife. I felt a
sudden urge to smoke a cigarette and for someone else to

light it. Since I chain-smoked all afternoon, that night I had to raise the blinds to keep from coughing, and the next morning when I got up the first thing I saw was that tailor waving to me from his porch. I yanked the blinds down so hard they broke, threw on some clothes, and beat it out of there like someone was chasing me. On the landing, coming up the stairs, were two men talking and laughing who went into Senyora Constància's apartment. She'd left the door wide open. The first thing I noticed on the street was that coffee-colored car, and then I realized it had been days since I'd seen it. All the way to the corner I couldn't stop thinking how that tailor must still be spying on me from his porch.

I don't know how long all this lasted. I was so drowsy at the café with the ferns that I didn't even feel like looking at the handsome man. I bought a newspaper, pretended to read it, and when no one was looking, I drew stars. I'd draw three at a time, with one point on the one in the middle stuck between two points on the one on the left and another between two on the one on the right. I couldn't stop smoking and hooking up stars. When I was home I'd look for photos. I was sure someone was leaving them there to drive me nuts and I'd look for them in drawers, in wardrobes, among my clothes, everywhere. I couldn't find any more but I walked by the hen without looking at it or just glancing out of the corner of my eye because I was sure they'd stuck one inside and I didn't dare to lift the top, not to keep from finding it but because I was scared of something or other.

Marc came every day but I never told him anything. One evening, when I was clearing the table after supper, he suddenly asked what I'd like him to give me when we broke up. I just stood there for a while, staring at him. He had the newspaper spread out on the table and on the last page there was an ad for jewelry. He started pointing to the jewels in the advertisement: there were ladies' watches, three or four diamond rings, a hairpin with pearls and some earrings. I told him the only jewel I'd like would be a diamond cross, but that it was something a loose woman would wear. He folded the newspaper, gripped my arms, and asked who the first one had been and where we'd done it. He asked me over and over, gritting his teeth so hard I thought he'd break them, and he was hurting my arms so much that out of desperation I told him the first thing that came into my head, that it was on Red Street, one night and any old way, with a man that I couldn't even see what he looked like. He let go and said that was just about right for a girl who'd lived in a shack, and the only person who could have told him was Paulina.

I peeked through the slats on the blinds. That coffee-colored car was parked outside. I thought I'd go crazy, and maybe thinking it meant I already was.

◈ **XXXVI** I WENT TO THE DOOR AND SAW ELADI. AS soon as we got to the dining room, Marc, who was sitting on the porch, pointed to me and said I'd been in love for a while. Chuckling, Eladi asked, "With you?" Marc raised

his glass to his lips, drank a few sips, and after a while said
he could tell if I was in love with him. And he said he'd
managed to arrange I don't know what and that he'd be
gone for two months, for real this time.

Instead of ending, all that craziness just kept getting
worse. Sometimes they'd knock on the front door. I'd run
to open it but there was no one on the landing. One night
around one o'clock, it sounded like someone had stuck a
key in the lock and was trying to open it. Screwing up
my courage, I went to look through the peephole but I
couldn't see anyone. I was so upset I went over to the door
leading to the other half-apartment and kept pounding on
it till my knuckles were bleeding. Then I went in the
kitchen, took a hammer out of the tool cupboard, and
started banging on the dining room wall. I thought Senyora
Constància would knock and complain or ask what was
the matter, but she didn't come. No one noticed, nothing
moved and that scared me even more than the noises. I
looked through the blinds at the tailor's apartment. He was
standing on his porch in shirtsleeves with all the lights on
so bright they hurt my eyes.

The day after Eladi came, when I got back from the café
with the ferns I found Marc sitting on the porch. I asked
him why he kept saying he had to leave but never did it
and what he was doing there all by himself. Instead of answering he muttered that I looked sick. When he was at
the door, he said he didn't like making love to a board and
things had better be different when he came back.

Eladi visited me a few times. He'd sit down, we'd chat

about this and that, I'd give him a liqueur and it seemed like he had trouble leaving. One day he said he had to take me out, I lived too cooped-up, and we went to have a drink and look out over Barcelona at the bottom of the funicular. Then he took me home, came up, stayed awhile, and before leaving kissed my hand, but a real kiss this time. It was a relief. I had a friend. That kiss rent the heavens and the next day I went to the café with the ferns and looked at the gentleman as calmly as I had at first. When I got home, it seemed like the hen on the sideboard was crooked and I picked it up to straighten it. There was a photo underneath. It was the sea, very dark with storm clouds up above, and in the middle, small and far away, a white sail. It must have meant death.

The next time I saw Eladi, he asked me to live with him. We were standing on a lookout on top of Montjuïc, leaning on a railing where you could see a bunch of shacks. My heart felt like someone had punched a tack into it. I just stood there for a while and finally whispered, "What about Marc?" He said he'd arrange it in the best possible way. He bought two suitcases, packed them, threw the pink dress in along with the necklace, and left the corset on the top shelf of the wardrobe.

I spent my first week at Eladi's place sleeping. I told him not to worry, that I had to catch up on a lot of sleep, that some nights I'd been so scared I'd spent them standing behind the dining room door. I was scared like a sick person, it was strange that I'd been so scared, someone had really had it in for me. When I started explaining all the things that had happened, Eladi cut me off and told me to have some more cognac. He'd hold the glass to my lips and I'd empty it. Eladi'd get into bed with me but nothing ever happened, and if I was still asleep when he got up, he'd tuck me in. Lots of times I'd open my eyes, just a crack, and see him staring at me out of that blue eye beside his patch. I wondered what the other eye was like under the black silk, whether it was full or empty. Whether it couldn't see much because there was a film over it or whether there was no eye at all because they'd taken it out and there was nothing but a socket streaked with red and pink veins. Ernestina, who'd been Eladi's wet nurse, was now his maid, his confidant, and everything else. She was tall, dressed in black with starched white collars. I walked around naked and didn't even notice it. If I got up to eat, I'd wrap a blue-and-white-striped bath towel around myself. You could say I just went from the bed to the table and the table to the bed, but one morning I felt like getting dressed and asked Ernestina if she knew where my suitcases were. She said no. When Eladi came back I asked him where they were. He said they were locked and he'd sent all my clothes to the laundry. A month after I got there I still hadn't gone out and couldn't because I didn't even have a pair of stockings. Eladi made me walk around a lot naked. He'd sit down on the bed, have me parade around and while I was walking he'd say my hips belonged in a museum. When he got tired of watching me walk back and forth he'd kiss my hand and say he didn't dare touch me because he was scared I'd tarnish. At suppertime he had everything brought to the table, sent Ernestina to bed, and made me eat naked, and when the first night I said I didn't want to do it he said at the beach it was even worse. Sometimes I thought about Marc like something dead and what he must have said when he found out his bird had flown the coop. But I thought it was all very weird. One night when I was lying half-asleep in bed, I ran my hand along my neck and remembered that pink necklace. The next day, after Eladi had left and while Ernestina was out shopping, I started hunting for my suitcases. The last room I went into was a study with bookcases up to the ceiling and a very pretty stepladder. On the wall at the end, behind the desk, there was a portrait. It looked so mysterious that it took my breath away. It was a girl with dark hair, cropped short and parted in the middle, with bangs over her forehead. She was sitting with her arms crossed on a table, her head on her arms, and, pouting a little, she was chewing on a pearl necklace. What fascinated me was her eyes, staring out with the pupils a little up and under those eyes she had two more just the same and you couldn't tell if she was looking with the top ones or the bottom ones or all four at once. Eladi came in, took my arm, and led me away. That night he made me drink three glasses of cognac.

The next morning as soon as I was alone I got up and started hunting for those suitcases again, but first I went in the study to look at that girl with four eyes and the first thing I saw was a photo on his desk. I picked it up and it took me a while to recognize who it was. In the photo I was leaving that café with the ferns in my pink dress. I forgot all about those suitcases. I spent the day lying in the easy chair with my feet up on the hassock, and that night even after all the cognac Eladi made me drink I still couldn't get to sleep. I went back to staying up all night and feeling worn out all day.

ॐ **XXXVII** THE COGNAC WAS TOPAZ-COLORED. Eladi poured me big glasses of it and then had me warm them between my hands. One night we emptied a bottle between us and by the end I couldn't see straight and the lights seemed to be twinkling. As I was falling asleep, I saw a flame flickering before my eyes, blue and lavender with a coral crest that looked like that flame Eusebi said came from dead people's bones. The next morning I woke up feeling groggy and told Eladi I'd seen a blue flame like a round passionflower. He told me not to worry, that for fun he'd burnt the little bit of cognac left in the bottle in a saucer.

After that night, when I was alone I searched for the bottle instead of my suitcases. I'd lock myself in the dining room and burn cognac in the dark. That flame like a dream brought back all kinds of memories. I hardly noticed that time was passing and I couldn't even remember what color the streets were. When I leaned back in that easy chair on the porch, wrapped in a towel, I couldn't think and didn't know what I was seeing. I lived on visions. I started having that dream a lot about the baby wiggling its arms, always the same; I'd keep that dream going from night to night and if I woke up and broke the thread, it would start in again where it had left off. I also dreamt about the cemetery, with Eusebi going around stealing flowers off the wreaths. Eladi kept making me drink. He wanted me to sleep, he said if I didn't sleep I'd die. Lots of nights he had to carry me to bed because I couldn't walk and as soon as I put my feet on the floor everything started swaying and once I screamed because it seemed like the floor had caved in beneath me. One night when he gave me cognac I slapped the glass out of his hand, I got up and somehow ended up on the back porch and collapsed like a sack throwing up. And then something started that I never could figure out if it was a dream or part dream and part reality.

Eladi's bedroom was very big; it had two doors onto the hall and the head of the bed was between those doors. A few days after I'd started living with him, I asked why his bedroom had two doors and he said it was because they'd turned two rooms into one. The bedspread was black velvet with a white fringe around the bottom. The curtains across the balconies covered the whole wall and were made of red velvet. The night I broke that glass, when I'd been lying in bed a long time, I half woke up and even though I was woozy I felt like someone was nearby. The doors were open and a dim light came through the first one. I had to shut my eyes because it was like I had a ball of fire inside me that was trying to burn through them, and then, with my eyes closed, I thought I'd seen Eladi standing by the door. And I don't know why but I thought it couldn't be him, even though, half in the dark, I'd spotted his black eye patch, but I'd have sworn that instead of covering his left eye it was covering the right one, and I couldn't remember clearly no matter how hard I tried. He did what he wanted with me. Then, instead of staying, he went out the other door, but what sounds so clear seemed blurry when it happened and the clearer I tried to see it the blurrier it got. A little while later a big shadow entered through the same door where he'd come in, pulled the sheet off me, and I felt something cold between my legs. When the shadow had left, Eladi came back through the door with more light and did what he wanted again. And the shadow and that coldness came back, and it seemed like the light from the dining room got brighter, like they'd turned on more lamps, and the big shadow's head was wrapped in a kind of purple turban. I felt something wet on my thigh and the cold made me shiver. Then Eladi came back, his breath stinking of cognac. I opened my eyes, it must have been the next day, and they felt so heavy that I could hardly keep them open. Eladi was sitting at the foot of the bed with a bottle beside him, and he gave me a drink. I started coughing and he slapped my back because what he'd given me was stronger than cognac. At suppertime I couldn't get out of bed. Ernestina left a little table beside the bed with a tray on it. I didn't eat much and neither did Eladi. Hardly knowing what I was doing, with no strength left in my hand, I pushed the tray away and rolled over. The shadow came back, with his head wrapped in purple. I stared at the folds in the curtain in that half light and all of a sudden the folds smoothed out and I started seeing the cemetery. The shadow began to get bigger, like it was growing out of the ground, till it hid the curtains from top to bottom and side to side. Eusebi and I were kids, everything was misty, there were niches half covered by cans of yellow and purple pansies. From time to time you could see folds in the curtains which twisted the things in front of them. Eusebi and I climbed some black ladders on wheels and shook them to make them roll forward; it was hard because they were so heavy, but I wanted to see if there were any names beginning with C on the wall with the niches. Before leaving, we stole some flowers and then threw them away because they smelled like death. And I felt the cold on my thighs, and we were back in the cemetery, and beyond it there was a meadow with a horse munching the grass. I brushed the pansies aside and next to them a flame shot out like a little tongue and everything was covered with wreaths wilting on the ground and black ribbons with gold letters half washed away by the rain. An angel who looked like Eusebi was watching me, and another angel tried to give me a bouquet of stone flowers. Some flames were running around frantically because they couldn't find the bones they'd come out of, time passed, and more time, and Eladi came and that reek of cognac, and the cold came and the light from the dining room got dimmer, and the cemetery melted away, and the curtain came back, and I stretched out my arm to touch my wet thigh and they gave me cognac and I didn't want it because the cognac wouldn't let me see what I wanted to see. The flames flickered back and forth and a voice said they weren't dead people, they were from the cognac, but sad and lonely, they flickered all around the cemetery and kept going in one door and out the other and fluttered around the foot of the bed. They came three times, because there were three of them, and even when all three did the same thing it was different, like faces you see going down the street that all have eyes and cheeks and mouths but no two mouths are the same and eyes are all kinds of colors and some cheeks are smooth and some are rough. Everything was different and it seemed like love was the difference between everything that's the same and one day when my brain didn't feel so heavy and my tongue didn't get in the way like a stone in my mouth, I started crying and asked Eladi what they did to me at night, what did they do? And he clasped his hands and said no one did anything, that I had to sleep to live. That he swore it. A little rat made of raw meat was trembling on my arm. Eladi brought me the glass and, half lying back, I drank the gold that was killing me. "You have to sleep" a voice kept repeating, and the baby in the dream wiggled its arms and we couldn't get those black ladders in the cemetery to move or read the names on the niches and a voice somewhere kept saying "You have to sleep" day and night and the cold between my legs and the shadow flitting in one door and out the other around the foot of the bed and I slit a vein on my wrist with a razor blade after making a cross on it and when I saw the quivering drop of blood I fainted. They brought me back to life and I was pregnant.

ঌ**XXXVIII** I KNEW IT RIGHT AWAY BECAUSE MY breasts felt sore. At that time, just hearing the doorbell or footsteps coming would make me shake all over. One night, when all that was left on my wrist was a jagged scar, Eladi woke me up, gave me a cup of coffee, and told me to get dressed because we had to go out. On the floor were the two suitcases they'd kept hidden. I couldn't understand it. I gazed at the suitcases and then at him without understanding, and he leaned over till his face was up against mine and said we had to leave, we had to go out in the street, and he kept repeating it, staring out of that bright blue eye beside the black silk till I told him to stop, that I'd gotten the message. He dressed me in that pink dress like I was a doll. Then he put on my shoes and left me sitting on the bed. All I wanted was to lie down because my brain ached and when he came back he found me stretched out. I saw him walking toward me and since he kissed one of his fingers and then stroked my cheek with it I thought maybe he loved me and started whispering that I didn't want to go, to let me be, that I was fine where I was. And I kept saying it till suddenly I felt them lift me up and found myself standing at the foot of the bed.

I had a lot of trouble walking on high heels. Eladi held my arm and led me down the hall and as we were going I turned my head and glanced at the two bedroom doors. Ernestina walked behind us with that starched white collar between her head and her black dress. She opened the door and Eladi pushed me into the elevator. Inside it smelled like hot irons, sweaty brass thimbles and damp woolen clothes. In the street they helped me into a car. I had to shut my eyes because the light from the streetlamps made my head spin and with my eyes closed I could feel how the breeze, which smelled good and a little feverish, made my dress flutter against my skin. When I opened them and saw where I was I tried to run but Eladi made me go in and said he always did what Marc asked him to, and he started making me walk up the stairs in front of him with his hands on my waist. I kicked him with my heel and then, without opening his mouth, he went ahead of me, grabbed my arm, and pulled me the rest of the way. Marc let us in, and the first thing I noticed was that the door between the two apartments was wide open. So scared I could hardly get the words out, I whispered that I wanted to go, that they should leave me alone, but they kept pushing me toward the dining room. Everything was like the day I'd left: the hen on the sideboard, the chairs against the wall, the cabinet up to the ceiling. The tailor was standing on the porch with his hands in his pockets and that self-satisfied look I couldn't stand. On the table were two photos and a little box tied with a gold ribbon. I felt dizzy and had to lean against the wall, but I couldn't take my eyes off that box because as soon as I saw it I was dying to know what was inside. Then Marc gripped my cheek with two fingers that felt like tongs, jerked my head toward him, and gave me a slap that echoed through the whole apartment. Eladi was standing by the dining room door, looking at us a little bored. My cheek started stinging and Marc pulled me over to the table, picked up a photo and shoved it in my face so close I couldn't see a thing. Then he put it back on the table and made me look at it; in the first one the general and I were leaving the café, and in the second we were going into his house. I grabbed them to rip them up but Marc knocked them out of my hand and they landed under the sideboard. And I started shouting at them to tell me what this was all about. And then the tailor, who'd been edging closer, put some other photos on the table and they were all like the one I'd seen in Eladi's study: me coming out of the café with the ferns in that pink dress. I covered my mouth and turned away so I wouldn't see them. And Marc started hitting me and I hit back and he told Eladi to grab my arms and Eladi didn't move so the tailor grabbed them and I could feel something digging into the back of my neck and I tried to break away and kicked them and shook my head and the harder I shook it the more that thing dug into my skin. They tore the chain off my neck, no one said a word, and Marc lifted my hair between his hands. I don't know how I had the strength to tear myself loose, run to the door and out onto the landing or how I managed to take those stairs four at a time without killing myself. When I was almost at the bottom, Marc caught up with me and we stood there for a while face to face, panting. Then he gripped my arm and when we were in the street he made me get in his car; Eladi and the tailor had caught up with us. I don't know where we went, it seemed like we were just riding around. Suddenly Marc said he had to rest because he couldn't see straight and he parked by the docks and we spent a long time staring at riggings and masts. A siren blew, almost right on top of us. My belly hurt; someone had jabbed his knee into it in the dining room. No one said a word, like the car was full of corpses. Then Marc slowly pulled out and we were back in the streets. You could hear a siren again, and another answering it from far away. Marc parked the car and, before getting out, the tailor ran his hand along my neck under my hair. We walked down badly paved streets, I was so sick I didn't know where I was stepping and all I could think about was trying to keep from falling. Marc shoved me from time to time, and twice he whispered for me to move. He left me against a wall that bellied out and when I heard him leaving, I turned and saw his back almost blocking the entrance to the street. Then I touched my neck and felt that little diamond cross.

$\mathcal{S}$ **XXXIX** I HAD TO HOLD ONTO MY BELLY; I FELT worse every minute. Drops of water fell on me from clothes hung out to dry. I saw a wide arched door with a rusty iron lock, and I don't know how long I leaned against it. A man went by pushing a wheelbarrow full of braided garlic and onions and didn't even glance my way. The tips of my fingers were stained with blood because I'd run them along my neck, which still hurt, and I started walking. One heel got stuck between two stones and I fell. Three soldiers were going by and one came over and helped me up and he was the first man who'd gotten that close to me without making a pass. With no idea of where I was going, I wandered through streets I'd never seen before and when I realized I was lost I must have already walked a lot because more people were up and about. When my belly hurt too much, I'd stop for a while and when it didn't hurt so badly, I'd start walking again. From time to time I'd stand in the entrance to some building and rest awhile, leaning my forehead against the door. I'd come out and raise my head so I could get a little air. I needed lines of trees with little leaves, trees belonged to everyone. The streets got busier and busier, everything was full of life and I was all alone and feverish. Soon I started feeling surrounded by photos. They made me feel like I was choking because they were different from the others: the people in them were alive, they opened and shut their eyes and moved their lips like they were talking. They were laughing. In one of the clearer ones you could see a woman in a summer dress with a cigarette in her lips and the smoke coming from the end of the cigarette made me dizzy. After I don't know how much time I smelled that scent and threw my arms around a lime tree. From that trunk I made it to a bench. I got up. I sat down again. I went from bench to trunk and trunk to bench like that was all I'd ever done. I felt like they were following me. They'd drag me back to the apartment. From bed to easy chair and easy chair to curtain, from red to black and black to red. Suddenly I felt such a terrible stabbing pain that I doubled over like I'd been cut in half. I stumbled but managed to grab another trunk and the tree smelled like lime-flower tea and lime-flower tea was to pour in cups and my fingertips were dirty with caked blood and the bottom of my skirt was dirty and soaked from when I'd fallen and the lime tree's aroma filtered down, of summer nights and sickness and the flowers sprouted from leaves that were their beds and that baby who was hurting me so much would come into the world with a face green as parsley, with a puckered lip and would sew and sew without a thimble and I told God it was His child and He should help me out. Like a great sense of peace, I felt a hand on my shoulder, my whole shoulder could fit inside that hand and a voice nearby kept saying something or other very slowly. A sour, bitter wave came up and I had to make a great effort to push it down because there were others right behind it and my head was splitting; I had chills and a fever and a warm drop ran down my face and neck. I felt some arms grab me and that's all I can remember.

✎ **XL** Sometimes I still think about that nun, with red cheeks like a peasant and delicate hands like a princess. While she was swabbing the skin where she was going to inject me, I'd look at her starched wimple. When she stuck the needle in, since she winced, I'd smile a little like I hadn't felt the prick and often I wondered why she'd become a nun. I didn't know where she'd come from or why a girl named Carmela took care of me, a little like Paulina but cuter, with her hair combed up, skinny as a rail, who must have been about eighteen years old. I could have made an effort to figure things out, but I didn't and all

I felt was sleepy. The last day the nun came, when she'd left, Carmela walked in with a rosebud in her hand, broken off at the stem; she said "Look, isn't that sad?" She told me there'd been a big storm the night before and when it was over she'd heard a nightingale that must have been lost and was singing by the summerhouse. She said they were going to come and install a phone because no one had lived in that house for years, and they'd put my bed on the porch because it was nearer the kitchen and got some sun in the afternoon. That same day when they'd installed the phone she told me the boy who'd come to install it had said he'd like to go steady with her and would wait for her in the square, because she said the front garden and gate led to a little square with a fountain and acacias all around it. I listened with half an ear, like her voice was coming from far away; she said she'd told the guy from the phone company that she was too young to go steady. And then she told me she had a sister, the second-oldest, who'd had to go out on the streets to make a living. And even though I might not believe it, when she'd read her mother's letter telling her what had happened she'd burst into tears. Maybe that was why she didn't like men. And why she didn't like anyone to touch her. Even when she was little she couldn't stand for her mother to comb her hair.

The house was white, as I found out later, old-fashioned, with a garden around it. With seven plane trees in front, old and tall, covered with leaves and spiny balls, the trunks spotted with green and yellow and dark brown patches. The back garden ended at a stream. There was a summerhouse, overgrown by a dying rosebush with tea roses, and two stone benches. The house had one story, with iron bars on the windows, and above each window, like half a garland, there were five dark blue carved roses.

Carmela couldn't believe I'd slept so many days at the clinic. She said they'd fed me through my veins, that they'd had a lot of trouble cleaning my blood. Softly and with a sad look in her eyes, she said I'd had a very rough miscarriage, that the doctor had told the nurse and the nurse had told her the first day she'd visited me like she was visiting a dead person. She also said I'd never be able to have kids and it might be better that way because the one I'd lost had something the matter with its heart that might have made it come out all deformed. And one day she came in looking very happy, opened a package, and holding her arms up showed me a nightgown. She'd bought me two, one pink and one blue, with embroidered cuffs and collars, and I don't know why but I thought the embroidery must have been done by girls in an orphanage. And she left, wearing her white-and-lavender-striped uniform with its crisscrossed straps on the back and a badly tied bow at the waist. And one evening, when she brought my milk and toast on a tray, while I was sitting up in bed she told me there was a gentleman who was very concerned about me and how one day she'd peeked through the keyhole because I was asleep and he was sitting beside the bed and she hadn't heard us breathing for such a long time that she'd thought maybe we were dead and that's why she'd peeked. "All I could see was your head," she said. "and twice he blocked it by running his finger along your eye-brow. When he leaves he practically tiptoes through the garden so the gravel won't crunch and you can see he hates to go and he always tells me to take good care of you. He gets in his car, gently closes the door, and starts it up. A car so big it can hardly get around the square, shiny as a star and coffee-colored."

XLI   I FELL IN LOVE WITH THE WALL FACING MY BED and the door in the middle of that wall. But more than the door itself, I started loving the doorway because that's where I'd see him come in. I remember it was the first day I took a bath. The bathroom was old, the holes in the gas heater were scorched and the bathtub wobbled. It wob-bled a little when I got in and I was afraid I'd fall over. Af-ter the bath I got back into bed. I still wasn't myself: my mind was fuzzy and it was like I did everything by instinct. The bath had worn me out and a great drowsiness came over me. All I know is two voices woke me up: one I didn't recognize, and the other was Carmela's little-girl voice. They came closer and all of a sudden I saw a shadow in the doorway. I covered my eyes because it seemed like I was seeing things again. Then I took my hand away and lay there for a moment with my eyes wide open: the man from the café with the ferns was at the door. And it all seemed very natural. He asked how I was feeling and I said I felt all right. And I think that's all we said. It was the first time he'd found me awake. Carmela had told me he came every day, very late, and he only went in to see me if I was asleep. So as not to startle me. When he'd gone I got up to watch him leave and went over to the window. His car was parked outside the gate. A coffee-colored car, Carmela had said . . . I breathed a sigh of relief. The car outside the gate was coffee-colored but it wasn't the one that had worried me so much when I was feeling scared.

Carmela and I brought the bed out onto the porch. The next day I had trouble waking up and couldn't figure out if I was in the shack or at the restaurant or had slept in a hotel room. I opened my eyes and the first thing I saw was Carmela up in a tree like a monkey tying two ropes around a branch. After a while she slid down to the first fork, put one foot on a ladder she'd propped against the trunk, slipped and fell to the ground like a sack. I hardly had time to feel terrified, because she bounced up again like a ball and went off carrying the ladder. She came back with a plank, ran the ropes through two holes at each end, knotted them, stood there for a while looking and tugging at them, and when she was satisfied she came running up to the porch windows and said she'd made me a swing.

I got up and went to look at myself in the bathroom mirror: that woman didn't seem like me. I opened a drawer in the dressing table and slammed it shut again like the diamond cross inside was a scorpion. I looked at myself again. I covered the bottom of my face and the sadness in my eyes was terrible to see. I went into the front room where I'd slept at first and stayed there for a while, not moving, looking at the doorway; I felt a kind of crazy urge to see

him right away, to see that shadow who'd saved my life. I
got dressed and went out and leaned on the railing around
the summerhouse, above the stream. A little water trickled
around the stones, and looking at that flowing water made
me feel a lot better. And smelling fresh flowers all around.
I thought of all the things that had happened. I remembered that white room with its bouquet of red carnations.
And the smell of medicines. I also remembered how they'd
asked me over and over where I lived and I'd told them I
didn't live anywhere. And that's all. When they'd taken me
to the house, Carmela and the nun had put me to bed right
away and I'd spent a few more days not noticing anything.
. . . Looking down at the stream, I suddenly felt like I
wanted to know everything and find out how I'd ended up
in that house. I started feeling chilly and went back inside.

He came when it was dark out and I took him to the
summerhouse. I'd had cigarettes in my pocket since that
morning but I hadn't smoked any. I opened the pack, tearing off the cellophane strip, held it out to him and he took
one and stuck it between his lips. I took another. He lit
mine, then his own, and as he did it I looked at his face
spotted with light and shadow. Very softly, because I was
embarrassed to ask, I said I'd like to know what had happened. In a calm voice he said a friend of his who recognized me from the café had seen me early one morning
sitting on a bench on the Rambla de Catalunya and as he
walked by I'd gotten up and grabbed a tree because I could
barely stand. He'd asked me what was the matter and I'd
fainted. A boy and a man who were passing by had helped

him to get me into a car. At first he'd planned to take me to a first aid station but I looked so bad that he'd taken me to a clinic run by one of his brothers. Later that morning he'd told everyone in the café about it. For days they'd been wondering what had become of me. When he found out I had no home or family, he'd gone to the clinic to see if he could help. He didn't say so but from his look I could tell he was very concerned. The day the doctor had told him I was out of danger he'd taken me to that house which belonged to him but no one had lived there for years.

The wind blew a lock of my hair loose and he tucked it behind my ear. Then he slid his finger down my cheek and let it rest in the dimple. You could hear the leaves rustling and the sound of little animals that come out at night. I felt like crying. I got up and walked over to the railing above the stream. When I felt him beside me I turned to face him, threw my cigarette in the water and when the red line had just sunk he put his hands on my waist and pressed it. I don't know how long we stayed like that, not saying a world. Finally he kissed my hair, said I still needed lots of rest, and left. It was like I'd known him all my life and had only known him. I ran into the empty room to watch him drive away. When I woke up the next morning, I found I'd slept with all my clothes on.

᠀ **XLII** NOTHING ELSE HAPPENED AFTER THAT EVEning in the summerhouse. And whenever he came we both acted kind of shy. It got cold at the end of fall and it was colder in that house because a lot of windows wouldn't shut tight. Carmela unlocked the front gate in the morning and left it open till nightfall so she wouldn't have to go out if anyone came. As soon as it was dark we'd go shut it together because we were both scared of that garden. Beside the gate there was a bell with a broken chain that rang all by itself when the wind blew. I liked it, and I also liked hearing the water in our stream after it rained. Carmela told me she'd asked for a couple of heaters because that house would be freezing in the middle of winter. A few days later they came to fix the boiler, and when it was fixed they sent two coal trucks. All we had to do was open our mouths to get whatever we wanted. And when Esteve— Carmela'd told me his name was Esteve—sat down across from me and asked what I'd done since we'd last seen each other, I looked at the side of his chest where his heart was and felt like touching it. One morning he sat down at the foot of the bed, next to it but like he was far away, because it was always the same with him. I never really had him, or maybe I did but didn't realize it. I sat up and reached out, and when my hand was next to his face, I ran one finger along the bottom of his cheek. I thought he'd vanish when I touched him because everything seemed so unreal. I laid my hand on the sheet and suddenly felt a tremendous urge to talk. He just stared at me. I told him how mandrakes scream when you uproot them. I talked about air and water and flowers and in the end I didn't even know what I was saying. He touched the scar on my wrist, looked into my eyes, and like he hadn't heard a word I'd said asked

"Why?" I didn't know what to say. I just thought how I'd like to always have him near me.

But even when he was nearby I felt like he was far away, like everything he thought and felt was bottled up inside him. He came and went, he gave Carmela money and maybe it would have gone on like that forever except that one afternoon when I'd been raking leaves in the garden I took a shower to freshen myself up. I had both faucets on full blast and the drain could barely handle all the water. I was standing in the tub with a soapy esparto glove in one hand, scrubbing my other arm, which was getting covered with little bubbles in all the colors of the rainbow. I didn't hear him come in, or maybe he'd been watching me for a while, but when I spotted him I didn't feel embarrassed at him seeing me naked. He stepped forward a little like he didn't dare to come too close, and when he was next to me I gave him the glove so he could scrub my back. He washed me slowly, without saying a word. It seemed like time had stopped. Then he carried me to bed wrapped in a towel and sat me down on his knee. I smelled like soap and water and felt cold, and my wet hair tickled my back. I felt like untying his tie and when I reached out the towel fell off. It was hard getting it untied. When I'd undone it, I slowly unbuttoned his vest.

I woke up early the next morning and it was strange to hear him breathing beside me. I put my hand on his heart. Then I took off his wristwatch, got up, and slipped behind the curtain. It was a cloudy dawn and there was a breeze blowing. I looked at the time; the watch had stopped at midnight. I wound it slowly and turned the hands back till they said six o'clock, the time we'd started loving each other. The minute hand seemed like death because it went faster and always passed the other. I held the watch up to my ear and then against my cheek for a while. The breeze under the balcony doors, which were latched but not shut, made me think of the little fan in one corner of the bar in that café with the ferns. I came out from behind the curtain, climbed into bed, and put the watch back on his wrist. It was hard to do in the half light. A little later I felt like pressing it against my cheek again and took it off him. The numbers glowed in the dark. I held it against my cheek and twisted his wedding ring around his finger for a while. Finally he woke up. I told him I'd turned his watch back. He grabbed my neck and pulled me over to him. And for fun I put my hand on his chest and asked "What's underneath?" Half asleep, he said "A pretty hand on a man's sun." I put my hand on his heart and asked "What's underneath?" And he said "A little hand on a heart." "No," I said, "a flat hand on suffering." I snuggled under the covers and put my hand on his knee and asked, "What's underneath?" Then he grabbed me under my arms and pulled me up and when my face was next to his he laughed and said "Bandit." I blew into his nostrils and said he was my angel. He squeezed me and stroked my hair and fluffed it up and searched for my eyes which must have been the only thing glowing in the dark and started caressing my face like he knew one day he wouldn't even be able to remember what it looked like. The sun didn't come up because it rained all day and that day was like a love feast. I remember it like it was yesterday. And how it ended.

⋑ **XLIII** ONE DAY AT THE BEGINNING OF WINTER, because a little girl had stared at me and laughed, I went crazy over children. I liked to watch them playing and kept some candy in my purse, but I never dared to give them any. I'd get soppy over them. A boy riding a hobbyhorse, a baby stuffing sand into an orange pail. A girl who opened her purse every so often and pretended to take something out and powder her nose, another who straightened her mother's skirt, a little one who kept tugging at her shoelaces. I liked them all. I kissed one little boy's elbow and it felt like a petal on a silk rose. The girl who'd looked at me was blond and wore a topcoat blue as her eyes. The nursemaid carrying her over her shoulder was walking ahead of me while the girl looked backward. I laughed and she buried her head, all gold, in the nursemaid's shoulder. When she raised it I made a face at her and she hid again and when she peeked out I laughed and she stuck out her tongue and squinted up her eyes, which were full of mischief, and laughed and held her arms out. Since I was walking slowly but the maid was hurrying along in spite of the girl's weight, soon they were far ahead and when they were pretty far away the girl waved goodbye with her little gloved hand.

When I wasn't looking at kids, I'd look at ladies, and whenever I saw one who was well dressed, elegant and refined with pearl earrings, I'd think she was Esteve's wife. The day I saw that little girl, I arrived home exhausted and freezing. I got into bed, and since I was bored, I started imagining I had a daughter, plump and with dimples on her hands. I made up the whole story, how I was married to Esteve, who Carmela'd said was an architect and that was all I knew about him because when he'd tried to tell me his life story I'd clapped my hand over his mouth and said I didn't want to know. And that day with the little girl, sitting up in bed, I waited for him to come home from work. I was dressed in one of the most beautiful nightgowns you could imagine, blue and filmy, with lots of lace and ribbons. The cradle was white and covered with ruffles, and the baby inside looked like it belonged to two angels. Then I imagined Esteve coming in and looking at the baby, who only laughed and never cried, and then he'd come over to the bed, sit down on it and it was like he was slipping away from me without moving, I don't know how to explain it, just smiling. He clasped my hand so his fingers entwined with mine. The rays of pale sunlight went through the gauze on the cradle and you could see all the cracks in the wickerwork.

I bought myself a wedding ring. I'd put it on when I was alone. I went to all the churches, praying that Esteve wouldn't get tired of me. I asked the flames on the candles and the wooden saints with thin hands. As I was coming out of church one day, I glimpsed Marc's car flashing by with him at the wheel and a cigarette between his lips. I felt a wave of anger boil up till it reached my teeth and was

so beside myself that for a while I didn't know where I was
or what I was doing. I don't know how, but I managed to
get home; I know I went through the gate, that the gravel
crunched beneath my feet, that I walked through all the
rooms and looked out all the windows at the garden like
nothing was mine anymore and everything was wrecked:
the trees turned to firewood and the house in ruins. That
evening I still was feeling jumpy. I went out and walked toward the sea, blindly, not even looking where I was going,
and all at once I found myself outside Esteve's building. I'd
walked there without realizing where I was going. The
concierge, who saw me standing at the door, asked if I was
looking for anyone in particular. Since I didn't know what
to say, I asked what apartment Esteve lived in and she told
me he and his wife had gone out quite a while ago and she
thought they'd gone to the opera. I found myself surrounded by people, while I just stood there. There were
two girls nearby, the nearest was wearing carnation perfume and was telling her friend all she wanted was to get
into the opera before she died, dressed like a queen. A fat
man pushed me aside so he could get by with his wife on
his arm. It was after they'd passed that I saw that white,
slender skirt, very smooth, on top of some silver sandals. It
was worn by a young girl with an hourglass waist and Esteve beside her as they came out holding hands. She
looked more like his daughter than his wife. She turned toward me and I glimpsed her cheek with a scar from her
temple to her neck. I bit my lip. Standing in the middle of
that crowd coming out, without noticing that he was

blocking them, Esteve stared at me like something from another planet. The next day when he came to see me, I started throwing up so violently that I thought I'd die. As soon as he entered the room, as soon as I saw him, as soon as he called my name even if he didn't come near me. As soon as he came through the door with that whipped-dog look I'd never seen on him before. God knows what I would have given to stop it. Because it was like I was dying burned up by love and vomiting.

◦**XLIV** A WHILE AFTER ESTEVE LEFT ME, A MAN around sixty years old came to visit, bashful and sadly dressed. He was wearing glasses and couldn't stop straightening them during the short time we were together. It was hard for him to get a conversation going, he said the garden was pretty, that he had his own house too but there were no old trees in his garden. Finally he took a piece of paper out of the inside pocket in his jacket and gave it to me to sign. It was a receipt for two hundred thousand pessetes. Since I looked a little surprised, he took a big sheaf of bills out of a briefcase with a lock on it and held them out to me. I took them, signed, and once I'd signed he asked me to please count them. I did, losing track two or three times, and finally he ended up counting them himself. Then he stood up and I saw him to the door. A week later I got a letter from a notary. Carmela and I wondered what he wanted. We went together. In the waiting room there was an etching in soft colors showing an old man in a bed with a canopy, and at the foot of the bed a gentleman was reading a document, sitting by a little table and surrounded by people of all different ages. Carmela and I agreed they must be the sick man's family. A girl who'd walked through a few times carrying pieces of paper showed us into the office, and the notary, after asking us to take a seat, said he'd summoned me so I could accept the deed to a house. I wanted to know what I was signing but I didn't even have to ask because another girl came in immediately and left a piece of paper on the desk and the notary read it to me: the house I had to agree to accept was the house I was living in. And that day my good luck began. But I couldn't have felt sadder. I cried a lot; Carmela said I'd go blind, that the tears would burn my retina. And I was seized by a tremendous urge to go out looking for Esteve and talk to him, even if it was only for five minutes, and tell him he'd done too much for me. I didn't dare to go to his house. Sometimes at dusk I'd walk down the street where he lived and stand there for a while, looking up at the light coming from his balconies. I thought maybe he'd open one and not see me and I'd call out but he wouldn't hear me. Finally, after thinking it over a lot, one morning I went to the café with the ferns. There wasn't one familiar face. The owner served me. I told him I used to come to his café every day because I liked those glass cases with ferns in them. He said now he remembered me and told me how before buying the café he'd taken a trip on an ocean liner and in the lounge there were glass cases with pressed ferns. He'd loved them so much that when he bought the café he asked the decorator to include some glass cases with ferns. And before I left he said he'd have to change them because they were so old and dry that lots of leaves had crumbled and the outlines weren't so clear any more.

I hid the two hundred thousand pessetes between the seat and back on an easy chair and gradually spent them without thinking they'd ever run out. Carmela, who'd decided to stay with me, one day said it was foolish to keep them like that, that I should put them in a bank and sell the house. That way I'd have an income, and if it wasn't enough to live on I could buy a tobacco shop. I told her I didn't want to sell the house, that instead of getting rid of it I was planning to have it painted. The painters found a little ivory hand on a shelf in the bathroom cupboard and we laughed because they said it was to scratch our backs with when we got old.

The house looked pretty, and Carmela and I especially liked the smell of paint which gradually faded away. I had irises and a lemon tree planted beside the stream. I spent lots of nights strolling through the garden, sitting in the summerhouse or twisting the ropes on the swing as tight as I could to see them unwind and watch the seat whirl around. One afternoon, when I'd just gotten out of the tub and was taking the last towel off the shelf, I saw that marble hand in the corner. It had a shiny wooden handle, almost black. The fingers were very nicely carved. I stroked my cheek with them, let them stay a while in my dimple, and ran them over my nose. I was standing there naked between the mirror and the blue afternoon. I opened my arms and inspected my whole body: my breasts weren't so budding, my belly didn't curve in as much. I went over to the dressing table, took the diamond cross out of its drawer, and hung it around my neck. Then I pulled the chair over to the mirror and sat down on it, with one leg on one side and the other on the other. Without thinking, I ran my hand over the eyebrows on that Cecília in the mirror. I stuck out my tongue and curled it up to see the veins that tied it underneath like purple snakes. I tapped the mirror with the hand, then slid it down to my knee. What's underneath? I pulled it away, then put it back on the mirror and left it in the middle of my neck. A little while later I stuck it under my breast, lifted it a little and asked the mirror how much each of my bones was worth. The belly doesn't count, the breasts are priceless, let's leave the heart out of it. I had to live until I died. A life has a lot of days in it. I pulled myself up to my full height and told that Cecília in the mirror she'd have to do something if she didn't want to die in a poorhouse and be buried in a pauper's grave.

⁊ **XLV** THE NEXT MORNING I FLIPPED A COIN. I CAME up heads. With that same coin in my hand, I called a florist and ordered some violets. I unwrapped them and, after pulling off all the leaves, I took some and stuck them in my hair on the side where I'd worn that pin Eusebi'd given me. I put on a gray dress and took my green snakeskin purse, which matched my shoes. And decked out like that, I went to call on Senyora Constáncia. There was no one in the concierge's lodge, but I hadn't climbed three steps before her husband's head peeked through the curtains in their apartment. I stopped short with one foot in the air, hiked my skirts halfway up my thighs, and, leaning against the bannister, asked "More?" The head disappeared.

The doormat outside the apartment where I'd lived was nice and straight. And Senyora Constáncia's was even more so. After taking a few deep breaths and calming myself, I knocked. It was a long time before I heard steps. Finally the peephole opened and behind it I saw a bit of Senyora Constáncia's face. She opened the door very slowly. Her eyes looked frightened and, without giving her a chance to say "Come in," I said "It's me, Cecília" and slipped through the door. Nothing had changed. That hat with artificial violets was on the stand. On top of the coffee table on her porch sat that blue slip, so carefully folded, with one broken strap. I inquired very politely about her health, her knees, her bad circulation and we sat down. Very calmly, I asked how Marc was doing. She couldn't stop staring at me. All of a sudden she wiped her neck, touched that dangling strap and said she didn't know a thing about him. She'd gotten over her surprise and let out a nervous little giggle. So she wouldn't realize I'd noticed, I gazed at the ceiling. The frieze around her dining room, like mine, was made of angels and pomegranates that I'd completely forgotten. I straightened my skirt and said I'd come because she had something I wanted: that

clock with the towers, which I'd like to buy. She looked at
me a little puzzled and said she'd never considered selling
it, that it was a family heirloom but in any case she'd think
it over. I looked out at the tailor's porch; the dummy was
still there. Without acting like it mattered much, I said she
should think it over carefully, that I wasn't in a hurry, and I
took a wad of bills out of my purse, held them for a while,
and then put them back. Her eyes followed everything I
did with my hands. The click from the purse echoed
through the dining room. She put her hand on her cheek
and stared at me like she was trying to read my mind. Her
hand fluttered and she said I'd put up with a lot. I told her
I didn't know what she was talking about and stood up,
took off my belt, pulled down the zipper in back, pulled my
arms out of their sleeves and let my dress fall to the floor.
Her mouth and eyes got bigger and you could see she
didn't understand. She straightened that slip, took a handkerchief out of her pocket, closed her eyes, wiped her lips
and whispered, "A treasure." Without realizing what she
was doing, she tugged at her own skirt. A few minutes later
I leaned over, picked up my dress, and put it on again. I
turned my back so she could zip me up. When I'd finished
I took the bills out of my purse and left them under the
slip, sticking out a little. As we were leaving the dining
room I turned and waved goodbye to the dummy, and she
couldn't have had any idea who I was waving to. In the
foyer I twirled the hat with the violets and, still looking at
them, said I'd be very grateful if she'd introduce me to one
of her nephews or some gentleman who was reliable, that I

didn't care what he looked like as long as he was good and rich. She acted very thoughtful and finally started talking like she was weighing every word. She repeated that I'd had to put up with a lot and that the others hadn't been so patient. That one of Marc's last few mistresses, a girl named Roser, tired of hearing noises behind the door between the two apartments, had called a locksmith who'd burst into her dining room while she was having breakfast, "Because I don't know if you realize," she said, "that your back porch has a door that leads to mine." Lowering her eyes and fidgeting with her collar, she said she hadn't done me any harm. What Marc had asked couldn't have been more straightforward: for her to keep an eye on his mistress and make sure she was faithful. That's what he'd asked the tailor, who'd been his friend since they were kids. That maybe, all together, they'd gone a little too far. She said if she looked in her drawers she could still find photos the tailor'd taken from his porch or in the street. How there was a brick near the bottom of the fireplace that you could take out and put back to hear conversations. I thought she knew a few things, I knew a few more, and between the two of us we didn't know the half of it. I told her I didn't care about all that and to think over what I'd said. When she'd closed the door behind me, I kicked her doormat so it was crooked.

◦ **XLVI** BEFORE LEAVING MY HOUSE TO MEET THE first nephew, I drank a glass of white wine. At first I'd planned to take a trolley, but after thinking it over I decided it would be better to grab a taxi. I knocked, Senyora Constáncia opened the door right away like she'd been waiting behind it, and, her eyes shining with excitement, she told me I couldn't have been more on time. She showed me into the living room: the sofa was upholstered with velvet, there were some easy chairs with doilies and the light came from a ring of china candles with little green cones above them. In one easy chair sat a young man who jumped up the minute we came in. Senyora Constáncia put it to him so straight that I didn't know what to do with my hands or where to look. And the young man, who wasn't as young as I'd thought at first, couldn't take his eyes off me and agreed to everything. His name was Ignasi. He gave me a down payment because Senyora Constáncia said I needed some security in case he got tired of me. And he set me up in an apartment. I dressed Carmela in dark gray glacé silk, an apron and a fine lace coif with a black silk bow that hung down in back. The apartment, which was very big and full of light, had two tiger skins on the floor and a zebra skin on the wall. Since I had money left over, I bought furniture for my house. When I was free I'd go and stay the night, and if I could spend a few days there I felt happy. I had them paint the outside white to show off the blue roses, and I had the front gate painted green. The painter asked if I wanted him to take the bell off and I said to leave it there, that it didn't bother me. Ignasi's face, chest and arms were covered with freckles and he was always asking me to stroke his forehead because he said my hand felt cool. I needed a drink before going to bed with him. Sometimes, without knowing why, I'd start feeling queasy, go to my house, and spend a couple of hours in the tub washing myself inside and out. This lasted three years. Three years of pretending I was in love. After three years, Ignasi said he was going to get married but everything could stay the same between him and me. I refused. I said married men were okay, but I didn't want a man who'd get married while he had me. Before leaving he said he'd miss me and if I changed my mind to tell him. I don't know what kind of nastiness that I didn't even know was in me made me wish him a lousy honeymoon.

I reached an agreement with Senyora Constáncia's second nephew in that same living room with the green cones on the ceiling lamp. He wasn't there when I arrived. He didn't come for another three quarters of an hour or so, and Senyora Constáncia was so nervous she kept wandering in and out. I tried to pass the time by looking at the clock with the towers. Finally he showed up. He was a small, thin man so clean he looked like they'd gone over him with a scrub brush. He also set me up in an apartment, but what he gave me to get started—Senyora Constáncia kept thirty percent—wasn't as much as with Ignasi, and he tried to trim it down even more. His name was Estanislau and he never used the main staircase. He'd take the servants' stairs, come in the kitchen door, and all the maids had the time of their lives. He didn't come very often because he said he had to preserve his strength and that he was taking a big risk. The less he came the happier

I felt, because that way I could spend more time at my house. I replaced all the windows that wouldn't shut tight, had all the leaks fixed, and Carmela put new ropes on the swing. When spring came, Estanislau said he had to go to Madrid on business and would take me with him. We hadn't been on the train two hours when he left the compartment, disappeared for a while and just when I'd started thinking maybe he was sick he came back looking terrified and said he'd run into a friend and had to join him in his compartment. He took his suitcases, and before we reached Madrid he came back and gave me a slip of paper with the hotel's address. I barely had time to unpack before he came in looking as guilty as if he was about to kill somebody and told me to take the first train back to Barcelona. I got so mad that he noticed and two weeks later when he came back, he gave me a tiara. I never could understand why when he handed me the box his mouth got like Cosme's, with that gold tooth.

❧ **XLVII** I was standing on Muntaner Street looking in a shop window when I heard someone calling me. It was Paulina, with a little boy. I hadn't seen her since we'd lived in that house with the irises, and she looked much worse. We were happy to see each other. She was sloppily dressed and it embarrassed me because everything I had on was brand new. She told me they'd spent the afternoon in Monteroles Park. We walked along for a while, not knowing what to say, and it didn't take long for me to realize something was wrong. I suggested that we go to a café and have a snack. Once we were seated, I asked if the boy was hers. She said even though we hadn't seen each other for years, it wasn't enough time for her to have a son that old. And she burst into tears. The boy threw his arms around her and started crying too. When they'd both calmed down, she said he belonged to the gentleman from Tarragona and his mother had died of cancer of the palate. As soon as the gentleman from Tarragona had been widowed, he'd asked her to marry him. She'd thought it over carefully and finally said yes. They'd gotten married secretly and he'd brought his son to her house, telling his family that he wanted to send him to school in Barcelona. But his brothers had found out and were ruining his life and wanted to take the child away because they couldn't forgive him for marrying someone he'd been seeing while his wife was alive and they told everyone how she'd not only been a servant but was a whore who'd gotten him in her clutches. The truth was that he was very rich and they all were dying to get his money. She said she'd kill herself if they took the boy away. That they loved each other more than if they'd been mother and child. The boy let go of her hand, which he'd been clutching the whole time, and touched my neck like he was looking for something. I asked Paulina what he was searching for and she said he must have remembered how once she'd told him she knew a gorgeous girl named Cecília who wore a glass heart on a chain around her neck. We talked for a long time. She wanted to know about Marc and I said I'd rather not discuss him. Since I felt sorry for her, I told her not to worry, that the gentleman from Tarragona was too rich for his family to take the kid; and besides, he was the father. She wiped her eyes and said yes, I was right, but they were trying to drive him to an early grave because he had a weak heart and if he died, five minutes later they'd get their claws into the kid. She started crying again, and so did the boy. When we were in the street we agreed to meet again. Since we'd been sitting for a long time and I was feeling kind of jumpy I walked up toward the Passeig de la Bonanova.

I'd been walking about ten minutes when I noticed a car following me: it was driving behind me very slowly by the curb. I didn't turn around. It was nice to think a car would follow me but it annoyed me too since I was starting to get tired and didn't dare to stop and wait for a cab because I was afraid they'd think I'd stopped to wait for them to ask me to get in. To make everything perfect, it had started raining. The headlights coming made the rain glitter and dazzled me. Two or three taxis went by with passengers in them. Finally, since it was raining harder, I ducked into a doorway. The car went by and just when I thought they'd leave me alone, it stopped. A uniformed chauffeur got out and invited me to get in. I didn't answer him. He got back in the car and then a gentleman came out and asked me to please do him the favor of getting in. It seemed the best way to get home quickly without being soaked. The gentleman was old, with gray hair, stunningly elegant. We saw each other a few more times and quickly reached an agree-

ment. I was especially glad to get rid of Senyora Constáncia, whose services were so expensive. His name was
Martí. He was involved in politics and he bought me an
apartment. The day I told Estanislau we were through, it
was like a bomb had gone off. He screamed at me to let
him have that tiara and the money he'd given me at the beginning; that I was breaking my word. I didn't reply and
just kept shaking my head. He said at least I should give
him half the money and the tiara. He said I could keep the
tiara but give him back the money. He said I could keep
the money but give him back the tiara. I kept shaking my
head. I must have acted so stubborn that with a murderous
look in his eyes he shoved me so hard that I fell on the
floor. That day he went down the main staircase.

XLVIII MARTÍ ALWAYS SAID HE WANTED TO SEE
me happy. To please him I put on perfume and makeup.
My skin was still smooth, but my face was changing, a little tighter around the temples and a little slacker around
the mouth. I spent hours looking at myself in one of those
magnifying mirrors and I knew my face by heart: the little
pimple that was taking so long to go away, the bit of fuzz
gradually turning darker, and the pink spot under my ear
that you could only see when I lifted my hair. In the afternoons I'd go out, sometimes for a walk, sometimes in the
car. I had a chauffeur named Miquel; and a real estate
agent, because Carmela'd finally persuaded me that the
best thing to do with my money was to buy an apartment

house. One day in an antique shop near the Plaça del Rei I saw a wooden angel tall as a person. I liked it so much that I went back to look at it a few times and bought it for my Saint's Day. When I got it home, I put it at the foot of the bed facing the headboard. Martí said I should stick it against the wall because you could see its unpainted back and it looked ugly. I didn't pay any attention to him. The angel looked at me like someone who'd suffered a lot. It was wearing a gold robe with a red band around the bottom and another around the neck; the folds in the wooden robe hid its feet and it had no hands. I liked to touch the rough edges around its wrists, where the hands had been cut off. It was the first thing I saw when I opened my eyes, and soon I bought another smaller one. I took the handless one to my house and told Martí I'd exchanged it for the other. I kept buying angels and having them delivered to my house. I had tall and short ones, with curls and straight hair, with goblets, palm branches, and grapes in their hands. I liked to go in my bedroom in the dark, with the starlight streaming through the window, and it scared me in a way that sort of kept me company. As if they were whispering my name. But they were silent, stiff, worm-eaten, earth-bound.

Martí gave me a diamond necklace like a river of stars. The day he brought it he sat me down on his lap. I felt so happy I blurted out that I'd bought a black easy chair. It was for my house, which was something he didn't know about. I wiggled out of it by saying I was waiting for it to be delivered and thought how now I'd have to buy another for the apartment. Martí said he couldn't understand how instead of saying something about the necklace all I could talk about was that easy chair. I laughed and hugged him. The necklace, which when I put it on had sent a chill down my spine, had warmed up so I could hardly feel it. He straightened it and while he was doing that he asked what I'd most like to have. Without even thinking I said I'd like to go to the Liceu wearing that necklace and see a lovely opera about a hunchback with his dead daughter in a sack. He laughed and asked what color dress I'd have made. I said red. A few days later he gave me a ticket to the opera. He said he'd be there with his family, watching me from their box.

The day I went to the opera, I spent the whole afternoon prettying myself up. Miquel waited for me outside the gate with his cap in his hand, and when he saw me he couldn't help exclaiming that I looked like a queen. We drove down the Rambla de Catalunya and, with my face pressed against the glass, I spent the whole time watching lime tree branches go by. Everyone stared at me as I entered. I walked slowly. When I reached the guards, I stopped a moment to catch my breath and pulled the bottom of my coat around me like I was afraid a gust of wind would catch it. A lady going in by herself, dressed in gray and covered with pearls, looked at me surprised because she couldn't understand why I was holding the bottom of my coat. I sat down where they told me to. I didn't dare to look around. I wanted to see everything, but without looking I knew I was surrounded by red and gold. I pretended to read the program but I couldn't even focus on the letters. I stared at a girl with a very high hairdo all covered with curls. I wanted to take my mind off Martí but I couldn't; I kept thinking how he'd said he'd be there with his family. And when I looked around he was the first thing I saw. He was in the third box from the stage, more elegant than ever, talking to a boy who must have been his son. His wife was dressed in honey-colored silk. I glanced away because I thought she'd realized I was staring, but slowly, dying to get a better look, I started watching her again. She had a cluster of diamonds on one side of her hair and a bunch of purple heron feathers stuck out of that nest of diamonds. The daughter was dressed in pink with flowers around her neckline. As the violins were tuning up I started to feel like crying.

The house lights dimmed. Someone came in late and the people coughing gradually quieted down. There was a moment of silence, and suddenly, like they were coming from another world, some very sad trumpets blew. When the curtains parted, the stage was brightly lit and full of jolly people. Men bustled around. They sure didn't look handsome: they had ugly, skinny legs and wore balloony pants in two or three colors that stopped above their knees. A younger one with a goatee, chubby and full of himself, was sitting there telling them about something in song while the others almost died laughing. The women wore sleeveless blouses with little vests, wide, wrinkly skirts and had their hair in nets. They weren't very pretty and most of them weren't young. But some of the dancing girls dressed as pages had very shapely legs. At first I didn't notice the old man with the little bells; he was standing quietly at the edge, so ugly it was scary. I started to feel bad: there was a weight on my chest like they'd piled something on top of it that wouldn't let me breathe. I didn't know what was the matter. I felt like my forehead was beaded with sweat, and I started worrying that I'd be sick. On stage there was a white-haired man, very upset, who was scolding the one who'd been sitting down singing at first. I closed my eyes, tired of watching, and realized I'd been fiddling with my ear like it was bothering me. I don't know why but I felt ashamed. I pulled my hand away and fingered that diamond necklace. The man with the goatee roared with laughter. I'd have liked to see the part that used to make Maria-Cinta cry, when the old man went by dragging that sack with his daughter in it, but I couldn't stand any more and left when the lights came on and everyone clapped. Before leaving I took a last look at everything: the bunches of lights that made the five gilded railings glitter, the round paintings on the ceiling, the big chandelier in the middle, the red curtain that kept opening and closing. Martí and his wife had gotten up and, leaning against the railing, they were chatting with some gentlemen. There was nothing of mine inside there and outside there were streets and air. I went out with my coat over my arm and couldn't see my car anywhere. Standing at the entrance, I felt the stares from the guards, burning into my back like the tip of a cigarette. I walked a little way up the street, then a little down it, and finally I crossed the Rambla. I saw my car outside a café, and inside Miquel was sitting at a table with a mug of beer in front of him. He leapt up and asked why I'd left so soon. I told him I felt like having a beer too. He glanced around and said it would be better to go to another café where we wouldn't attract so much attention. And he was right: with such bright lights and so many staring faces I felt embarrassed about my red dress covered with strings of beads, my stiff silk coat and gold net handbag with diamonds and rubies on the clasp. I got in the car and told Miquel to drive to the Rambla de Catalunya and stop under the first lime tree.

I took off my tiara. When he'd parked, Miquel asked if I'd like to go someplace and have a drink and I said no, to wait for me at the Diagonal because I wanted to walk up alone. And I started walking. The night was dark and I looked like a drop of blood. I walked slowly, swaying a little because I liked the sound the beads made. That sick feeling I'd had at the opera had gone away. I felt right at home under the lime trees. I thought how surprised Martí would be when he saw my seat empty. I felt like whirling around fast with my arms out, like I'd done when I was a little girl and wanted to see the earth spin. But some people were coming so I stayed where I was. I waited for them to pass. When they'd gone, I felt a little dizzy and sat down on a bench. "Your womb will get chilled" that woman at the restaurant had said years ago when I'd told her I sat on stone benches by the street. A few cars roared by and when they'd passed I heard a voice right beside me saying "Cecília."

ᴐ **XLIX** I COVERED THE CLASP ON MY HANDBAG BE-
cause I was scared whoever it was would steal it. The voice
asked, "Don't you recognize me?" I turned a little and saw a
man sitting beside me who at first I didn't think I'd ever
seen before. His cheeks were sunken and he looked like
he'd just escaped from a graveyard, with dull eyes in black
sockets like on a skull. There was a huge black spot on one
side of his forehead. He asked if I really didn't remember
him and without waiting for me to say it, he said he was
Cosme. You couldn't hear even a leaf flutter. He'd started
off whispering like he was praying but his voice soon got
louder and he kept telling me how much he'd suffered. He
said maybe there were men who'd loved me, men who'd
been able to tell me so, but he was the one who'd loved me
most of all. His voice trembled like it was hard for him to
get it out and I wished I was buried so the earth would
muffle that voice. . . . What had become of me, that was
the only thing he'd wanted to know: what I was doing, how
I lived, who I was living with. That if I'd gotten in trouble
he would have helped me out. He'd worked hard, gotten
rich, and had the best hotel on the Costa Brava but he
didn't know what to do with all the money that kept piling
up. He still lived behind his restaurant, with the glassed-in
porch and the sink and that engraving of the horse above
the table. Just like before. He kept the black satin dress I'd
worn on Midsummer Night wrapped in tissue paper. I
turned all the way around to face him and saw his gold
tooth glittering. He'd also kept the medallion with the lady's head from olden days. If I wanted to see it all for my-

self. . . . He kept edging closer, he slipped his arm around my waist and I shrank back a little. He looked at me like a starving man looks at a table heaped with food. I pulled away. My skirt stretched and one of the strings of beads must have snapped because when I lay my hand on the stone a few beads dug into my skin. I didn't know what to say or do and felt a weight in my stomach like I'd swallowed a stone. He sat there for a while without speaking; he'd pulled his arm away, and just when I thought he'd finished he started talking again.

He hung his head and it was like he was talking to himself. I don't know what he said, that he'd wanted to see me, that to keep from bothering me he'd never spoken to me before. How the child we'd had—I felt the flesh crawl on my cheek like it was covered with ants—had been a girl. The doctor had told him not to cry over it, that we'd have others. It seems he'd stumbled out of the clinic so upset that he'd had to lean against the door awhile and even though he'd done his best not to think about it he'd seen her all the way back to the restaurant. He hadn't been able to sleep that night. When I came back, feeling better, every time he looked at me he'd see that girl dead before her time who tied us together because she'd come from both of us, and when he realized it was goodbye forever Cecília he'd had a friend do a sketch in sepia of a little girl; he'd told him how he wanted her, with curly hair, sitting down, and he'd asked him to print my name in pretty letters under the drawing. And he said that through some kind of mystery the girl in the drawing looked a little like me, as if I, who'd been his woman, had become his daughter in that sketch. And he'd put earrings on her: two nice little rings. And a bracelet. . . . That stone kept getting heavier inside my stomach and the beads dug into my hand and I wanted to get up but I couldn't. He said he'd put the drawing in a stand-up oval frame under the horse, and when he got sick of doing his accounts he'd sit there for a while, looking at it. He was resting his elbows on his knees and his knees were apart; he stared at the pavement like he'd dropped something and was looking for it and talked very slowly, saying the girl in the drawing had her hands in her lap and was wearing a pleated skirt and shoes with bows on them.

He stopped talking, and maybe because he wasn't looking at me I brushed the beads off the bench and without realizing it I stood up. I started walking, the way you feel when you're walking in a dream, and when I'd gone about fifty steps I don't know why but I felt like I was being followed. Without thinking I lifted my skirts and started running. One of my shoes fell off, I stopped to put it on again and also had time to glance down the street. A gentleman and a lady had stopped and were facing me, and some guys were talking on a bench. You couldn't see anyone else; lots of light was coming from the corner and the two rows of lime trees almost met in the distance. I got in the car at the Diagonal and when I could talk again I told Miquel to take me to the house instead of the apartment. I leaned back, then sat up, opened the no-draft window to get some air and with my hands over my mouth I closed my eyes because the buildings and trees flying by made me dizzy.

The car went around the square and when I'd gotten out Miquel asked if I wasn't scared to walk through the garden by myself. I told him I didn't think I'd ever be scared again. The car drove the rest of the way around the square and left. I slowly walked over to the summerhouse, sat down on a bench and started smoking a cigarette with my eyes closed. When it was half finished, I tossed it into the stream. You could smell the greenery. The sky was pitch black and every star looked like a tuberose. I can't remember anything else; I was standing by the balcony on the porch with my forehead against the glass and I must have stayed there a long time because it was starting to get light. I lay down on my bed with all my clothes on and fell asleep. When I woke up I felt a little sick and to get the bad taste out of my mouth I went and made myself a strong cup of coffee. I didn't start feeling all right till I was in the tub; I clamped my big toe over the faucet and sprayed everything. The water made little ripples that lapped against my neck and shoulders and I wiggled my toes so they'd keep coming. And I didn't want to get out.

I went back to bed wrapped in a towel but before climbing in I picked up the dress, which I'd slung over a chair, and hung it up. There were beads all over the sheet and I absent-mindedly started brushing them off; some were hidden in the folds. I took a sheet of paper off the night table, rolled it into a cone, and picked them up. First the ones on the bed, then the ones on the floor, kneeling. They looked like aniseed.

L . . . LIKE THE ANISEED THE NIGHT WATCHMAN used to give me when I was little. I slipped into bed but I didn't stay there long. I got dressed and can still remember how when I reached the garden I had to go back because I needed the money in my purse to grab a taxi, and everything I did till I found out where that old man lived, and how long it took me to screw up my courage to knock on his door. Looking at the stunted geranium in his window, I asked if he remembered how he'd found me. He looked at me and I looked back, he was very old, like that old man with the bouquet of roses, and he was sitting by the window in a corduroy suit, with the wales going in and out, the top button on his shirt undone, woolen socks flopping around his ankles, bushy eyebrows, his eyes still bright, between hazel and dark green like on the old man with the roses, peering at me as he tried to remember. I clasped his hand and held the tip of one finger in the dimple on my cheek. "I'm Cecília. Don't you remember?" I'd had a lot of trouble finding out where he lived, I'd hunted all over Barcelona, the neighbors around the house where he'd lived when I was little hadn't been able to help much, some didn't know a thing, others recalled that he'd lived in Sants with his son, but they didn't know where, and he hadn't settled down till he'd moved in with his daughter, because his daughter lived in the same neighborhood where he'd been a watchman. And the gardener, who'd been the first person he'd gone to see because he lived across the street, had died years ago and there was a garage where his nursery had been. But his son was also a gardener and the old man with the roses worked for him. He was sitting on his front step, wrinkled as a prune and with a cigarette wet with spit dangling from one corner of his mouth, and just when I was thinking how too much time had passed and nobody remembered, he said he knew where the son lived and I went straight to see him and found him eating lunch, and he told me where the sister lived and that her father was still with her, and so, from one to the other. . . . I asked if he remembered finding me. He shook his head like he really didn't remember, but his eyes glistened from wherever it is tears come from, and suddenly he told me to go home, that they were dead and I should go away.

The house was very sunny, painted pink. The bedstead was made of iron and at the head there was a picture of Jesus Christ with the Sacred Heart surrounded by saffron-colored light that gradually turned sulfur-colored around the edges. The old man looked dead, and after a long time he said, in a voice that seemed to come from far away, that I was whimpering and the dog was almost on me. The picture held up one hand with two fingers out in blessing, and there was a rip like a big button hole so you could see the heart crowned with flames. While I was looking at the Sacred Heart, the old man asked why I'd come and it was like he was scolding me, like it made him mad to see me. I was going to explain how I'd had a miscarriage a while back . . . that a string of beads had broken, and the beads. . . . But I thought he wouldn't understand so I didn't bother. And to say something, since I didn't know what to say, I talked about Senyor Jaume and Senyora Magdalena. Then, with a very innocent look on his face, he said he'd switched houses, that I'd been left on Mrs. Rius's step but he'd thought with her boys so grown up what would she do with a babe in arms, a newborn child. . . . I don't know why I asked if he'd seen anyone, if he'd seen what whoever had left me had looked like, and he said at first he'd thought it was a burglar and I was a bundle of stolen goods till he heard me cry. The guy ran like the wind and when he was far away he doubled over like someone had kicked him in the stomach. He was throwing up. But he hadn't thought about it till afterward because if I hadn't started whimpering and if he hadn't spotted that dog sniffing around he would have chased him, since it's better to catch a thief than recover some stolen goods, but he heard me and saw the dog and ran to scare it away before it hurt me.

I heard steps, and his daughter came in with two cups and a teapot. "It's lime-flower tea." She told me her father was so used to staying up all night that he couldn't sleep unless he had some lime-flower tea in the evening. I said maybe he missed seeing the stars. He shook his head and whispered, "The smell of flowers." A while later he said he was cold and asked me to give him a white silk kerchief that was folded at the foot of the bed. I picked it up and felt like tying it around his neck but he took it, rolled it up, put it on and tucked the ends into his shirt. Everything smelled like a sickroom and I couldn't have felt happier. While he was drinking the tea he told me how one day they'd thought I'd gone out and gotten lost because they hadn't seen me for a long time and had searched all through the house till Senyor Jaume needed some tools and found me in the shed, sitting on a pile of sacks wearing Senyora Magdalena's rosary like a necklace, and through the half-open door he saw me kiss the cross every so often. And that had made them want to dress me up like a nun. It was a dumb idea because from then on I always wanted to dress like a nun and when they took my habit off I'd scream that my bones and head were freezing.

There were bits of lime flower in the bottom of my cup. I stirred the sugar with my spoon and he stared at me, half-hypnotized. He said if I remembered how lime-flower tea had tasted when I was young I'd realize this stuff was worthless. What I'd drunk before was from the lime tree in the garden behind the house where he'd lived for so many years, and the gardener'd always told him he'd never seen a tree like that one, which must have been two hundred years old and was two stories higher than the roof. He'd spread a sheet on the ground so the flowers wouldn't get dirty and when he came for his monthly pay and brought me aniseed he'd also bring a bag of flowers. He stopped like he was trying to remember something and then said the petticoat I'd worn under the nun's habit had been sewn by his wife, who made lingerie, with the bodice covered with thin pleats. He asked if I like lime flowers and I didn't know what to say. He said it was a very pretty flower: a few flowers on a piece of silk and when you brew it up it makes you drowsy. He glanced over toward the window and said he still hadn't gotten used to not being out all night and

seeing people come home so sleepy they could hardly
walk. And so many keys and doors. . . . And slowly, in a
whisper, I asked if he could remember what he looked like.
A little puzzled, he asked "Who?" And I said, "The guy who
left me on the step outside the gate." He was silent for a
while, staring off into the distance, and just when I
thought he didn't even remember what I'd asked him he
repeated that he'd run like the wind; that when he'd seen
me he immediately figured I was an abandoned child and
had picked me up, holding me against his chest because
he was afraid I'd fall, and I was whimpering like a kitten
with my puny little voice, blinking my eyes and staring
though maybe I couldn't see a thing. The first thing he'd
thought was that they'd like to have me. It made him feel
good to leave flowers by their graves. He could still remember the first time he'd visited the cemetery. He remembered it so clearly that if he closed his eyes he could
see it all like he was still there. He was walking up the road
with a crowd of other people; a lot of them were carrying
bouquets of purple irises and others had everlastings.
Since he was tired from climbing, he'd turned around and
seen more people with bouquets of irises that looked like
purple butterflies, and between the kind of light from that
rainy afternoon and the winding road, it looked like a purple river climbing upward. He always took chrysanthe-
mums and white roses, never carnations. And that first day
in the cemetery he couldn't find their niche. He was
searching for their names and while he searched he remembered what they'd told him, that your last doctor, to

make sure you're dead, pokes your heart through the ribs because more than once they've buried people alive. He'd asked a man who was standing on a ladder replacing some flowers if he knew where their niche was, and that man had told him to ask a gentleman at the gate who had a book where it was all written down. The gentleman at the gate had quickly found their lane and number. He'd left the flowers and gone home. He'd thought of how when I was young I'd been so much trouble, always trying to run away. Afterward he'd visited both of them in the cemetery till he realized that dead people didn't stay put. He said that, sitting in that chair, some days he imagined himself dead. He was leaving the cemetery, stretched out on a wagon and between his feet he saw the horses' ears and the smell of flowers wafted up to him because since the wagon was floating three feet above the ground and it was always spring, all the smells from the gardens got into his nostrils. And many years later, he said, you stop traveling on a wagon and wander through the streets like a ghost doing what you'd done when you were alive, and if dead people's bodies were solid like ours we wouldn't even be able to cross the street. . . . He looked at me like all of a sudden he'd noticed that I was listening, and in a changed voice said he'd comforted them as best he could, and that urge to run away had come from a bird that, when we'd transferred it from the cage where we'd trapped it to the cage where it was going to live, had rammed its head between the bars for two days and two nights to push them apart so it could fly away. They'd found it lying belly up with its

head on the metal floor and its beak covered with blood. I
kept the cage beside my bed with a stone I'd put in it, saying the bird was inside that stone. You could see I was very
odd. With the bird I'd found out that everything has to die
and since they'd told me how when someone dies everybody wears black, I asked them to dress me in black and
whether when people were buried they buried their heads
too, and I held onto my head like I was afraid it would fall
off. And that nuttiness lasted a long time, as long as the
other business about not letting them take off my nun's
habit, and I kept saying I didn't want them to bury my
head: that I didn't mind about my arms and legs, but not
my head: that they should cut it off and stick it in a box
and keep it forever. . . . Once I'd left, they almost never
talked about me, but they kept everything like it had been
and Senyora Magdalena made my bed every morning and
turned the covers back at night. They never tried to find
me. They said if I got into trouble I'd let them know, and if
I'd run away for good they'd rather let me go and not try to
keep me there by force. Gradually they started talking
about me like I was still living there: that my appetite was
bad, that I liked black cherries and almonds, that I was a
fussy eater. One day they had a quarrel over a hairpin,
which must have been the one Eusebi'd given me and then
they'd taken and hidden it, and it was like they thought
that whoever had it could bring me back by squeezing it.
When they'd stopped talking about me, Senyor Jaume had
his bed brought up to the tower and shut himself in, and
she lived downstairs with the cats, because the cats Senyor

Jaume and I had managed to scare away by yelling from the roof and pouring buckets of water on them and coming out with a rag fluttering on the end of a broomstick had gradually come back. Occasionally Senyor Jaume would come out at night and give him a chair, but less and less because ever since he'd shut himself in the tower he'd left it inside the gate so he had to come in and get it. Senyor Jaume said the tuberoses wouldn't grow right because of the cats. Senyor Jaume died in the tower, and he and Mrs. Rius's oldest son brought him down tied to a chair they had to hold up between them. Mrs. Rius's son went in front and he walked behind so his share of the weight wouldn't be so heavy. When Senyora Magdalena was all alone, everybody wondered what she'd do, and she went and lived in the tower just like he'd done. The house got so run-down that sometimes you thought it would collapse. While he was still alive, Senyor Jaume had fixed the leaks but finally he'd given up because as soon as he went out for a walk she'd go up on the roof with a hammer and wreck everything he'd done.

He brushed one of his eyes because a very long hair on one eyebrow had gotten in it, and I looked at the sewing basket beside my chair and saw some scissors sticking out among the spools and balls of yarn. The sunlight, which at first had only touched the foot of the bed, had crept up to the pillow. He said once Senyora Magdalena was by herself, it seemed like there were even more cats and they made a tremendous racket, especially at night. No one dared to complain, but to shut them up the next door neighbors brought food from time to time and left it by the flower bed with the lilies. And all of a sudden it seemed like there weren't so many cats around and the people with the food said something stank and a rumor spread that she kept cats inside the house. When she died and they went in, they found a hole in the kitchen ceiling, a hole big enough to see the sky through it, and the floor tiles were loose because you could see all that rain had gotten under them. They couldn't understand how she'd managed to walk across the roof every day to reach the tower without bringing the whole house down. On the bottom shelf of the kitchen cupboard there were some dry bones and two dead cats. It seemed like she'd killed them. They found at least a dozen more at the bottom of the well, which had gone dry. The stench came from there. Of course she was broke. The people holding the mortgage hadn't seen a pesseta in years, but they were kind-hearted and had waited for her to die before taking over the house. The house didn't last long. Two months later they sent a steam shovel, and the next thing you knew there was nothing left. The lemon tree went too. And leaning forward a little, he asked "Don't you remember that lemon tree?" And it was like he could still see it. One night, when I was six or seven, the wind had cracked a branch and early the next morning they'd sent me to buy raffia at a shop which made straw mats so they could tie the branch and bind the wound. He and Senyor Jaume had steadied the branch with a pitchfork and pushed it up near a thicker branch. They'd stood there for a long time holding that pitchfork and waiting for me to show up and when I finally came back I didn't have the raffia. I said the shop hadn't opened yet and I'd been waiting for them to come. But the grocer's wife had already told them how she'd seen me on the trolley tracks and gone over and asked what I was doing and I'd said I couldn't understand why the tracks were apart there but came together at the end. Senyor Jaume was ready to kill me. Luckily some neighbor's kid had passed by and they'd sent him to buy the raffia and had managed to bind the branch and tie it to the other one. And the branch survived and bore lemons as juicy or juicier than the ones on the branches that had always been okay. He'd bought them both flowers every year till they'd made him retire from his job because he'd never wanted to ask his kids for handouts. It was then that he'd realized that after a while dead people leave the cemetery.

He brushed his eye again and said without looking at me that all those dead souls made a cloud of love, because love. . . . I asked him, "What about love?" I felt like pulling up his socks; you could see a patch of leg with a purple sore and the tissue must have been too old to heal. And I imagined him like he'd said he imagined himself: stretched out on a flying wagon drawn by black horses through streets he knew by heart. . . . I thought I'd like to be put in the same niche, with his bones pushed aside so mine could fit too, and maybe at night we'd be one flame and go crazy in the cemetery lanes and under those cans with purple and yellow pansies, or else we'd keep still, locked inside someone's memory. He brushed his eye

again and I looked at the sunlight creeping up the pillowcase and told him I'd fill his window with geraniums because the one he had was dying. He said no because then
he wouldn't be able to see the people going by. Then I said
I'd buy him a sweater if he'd tell me his favorite color. He
said no because his daughter made his sweaters out of
such thick yarn that no machine could knit it. I said I'd buy
him a cockatoo. He looked at me a little worried and said
no, they can give you a sore throat. I laughed and said "Yes,
I'll buy you a cockatoo and every time I come and keep you
company we'll make him so mad he'll start swearing and
then we'll give him lime-flower tea." He felt so happy he
started laughing, like he was laughing all by himself. When
he'd stopped he put his hand on my knee and then, chuckling, he asked "What have you done with your life?" I was
about to tell him I'd spent it searching for lost things and
burying dead loves, but I didn't say anything and acted like
I hadn't heard him, and after a while he took his hand off
my knee and asked if I'd been lucky. "See?" I said, "I've got
a star on my hand." He sat very quiet for a moment, like he
was thinking something over, and then he blurted out that
he'd like me to give him a rosebush. Like the one Senyor
Jaume was carrying against his shoulder one afternoon
when he'd seen us through the blinds leaving the nursery
while he was getting dressed. A rosebush round like a ball,
the kind that has clumps of roses and each clump always
has buds and flowers and is always in bloom. I asked him if
he meant the kind with pink roses. He said no, there were
white ones too. I said "No, pink ones; dark pink when

they're buds and pale pink when they're open." I looked around and it seemed like the ceiling was higher, the window was bigger and he seemed taller too like he'd been growing while we talked and I hadn't noticed. Everything was bigger and I was smaller. I put my feet on the rung under the chair, with my elbows on my knees and my face in my hands. I said very slowly, "I'll buy you a rosebush, a thick wool sweater, a cockatoo and aniseed . . . bushels of aniseed." He roared with laughter and brushed away two hairs that were hanging over his eye. I asked if he wanted me to trim them. He gave me a kind of look like he wasn't looking and then started laughing. I laughed too and it was like I was getting younger and younger. His eyes shone and his cheeks were flushed from so much laughing, and I saw the patch of sunlight, which was off the pillow and had started creeping up the picture with the Sacred Heart, and we laughed so hard that tears came to our eyes and when he'd caught his breath he said he knew why he was laughing but I didn't and I'd never guess. I said maybe the lime-flower tea had made us drunk and he said yes, on white roses that are one color when they bud and another when their petals fall off. He said one summer when I was around six or seven they'd brought sand for the garden and the whole garden had smelled like the sea. He cleared his throat and asked if there was any tea left in the pot. I poured him what was left and between slurps he told me he'd remembered something, and he repeated about how they'd brought sand for the garden and the whole garden had smelled like the sea and the smell reached the street.

It was stiflingly hot. He'd rung for his chair and it seemed like they'd never come out. Finally Senyor Jaume and Senyora Magdalena let him in and said "Hurry, come and see how she's sleeping." They left the chair where it was and went in. The doors and windows were open but there wasn't the slightest hint of a breeze, and the house smelled like fried fish and from the front hallway he saw the table set in back and the lamp lit above it covered with mosquito netting and everything was very clean, so clean he was afraid he'd get the floor dirty because they were both in such a hurry that he hadn't wiped his feet on the doormat. They stopped in front of my door and Senyora Magdalena shushed them and they stood there for a moment listening. Then they all tiptoed in and Senyora Magdalena turned on a yellow night light beside the bed. I'd thrown the covers off and was lying with my back to them, hugging the pillow. Senyora Magdalena cupped her hand to her mouth and whispered, "I feel sorry for the guy she marries!" And they laughed. I was wearing a white kerchief around my neck because I'd had a sore throat and before putting me to bed Senyora Magdalena had given me a thick slice of toast soaked with hot vinegar. "Your arm was shiny," he said, "and the light cut you in half, with one half white and the other yellow." I must have felt something strange in my sleep because I turned my face toward the ceiling, still clutching the pillow, and he stared at my open mouth because a sleeping person's mouth had always bothered him. They burst out laughing and I woke up and glared at them like they were thieves in the night; I sat straight up and pulled the sheet, which was crumpled up at the foot of the bed, over me. Then I pulled my legs up and started groaning because I had a cramp in one leg. I held onto my thigh and shook my head from side to side and he told me if I could lay my foot flat against the wall, that sometimes the coolness would make the cramp go away. And it must have worked because all of a sudden I dropped my foot, hugged the pillow again, and you could see I was hopping mad.

They went out, roaring with laughter, and they couldn't stop. That night, listening for the sound of clapping hands, sitting beneath the branches from the olive tree next door with the back of his chair against the wall, he kept thinking how happy it made them to have me there and watch me grow up, and how quickly time flies.

Then he kept quiet for a while, thinking about something, and he started laughing again. . . . He told me he'd named me himself. That when he was a kid he'd been madly in love with a girl who lived nearby named Cecília. She was always sick and finally she died. The day they took her away to be buried, her mother came out of the house frantic, with her eyes all red from weeping, and spreading her arms she cried "Cecília, Cecília!" While he was shifting me from one step to the other he thought they ought to give me a name and it would be nice if it was Cecília Cecília. He'd walked over to a street lamp and seen that I was a girl because my ears were pierced. A little nervously, he took a scrap of paper out of his pocket and stood there wondering what to do; he put me down on the ground again, looked to see if he had any string but even though he always carried some in case he needed it that night he didn't have any. Luckily I was wearing a bib fastened with a safety pin. He wrote Cecília once and when he was about to write it again a window flew open and he got scared. He dropped his pencil and couldn't find it. He undid the safety pin, wetting his fingertips with the drivel on the bib, and fastened the bib and the paper together. Since no one was around, he rocked me awhile, whispering, "Cecília," and I laughed. Then he rang the bell and gave me to them. While he was undressing, his wife woke up and asked why he'd come home so late. He told her he'd found a baby girl. And she asked "Where?" And he said, "Halfway down Camellia Street, outside a gate with camellias all around." His wife acted like she didn't believe him and he had to re-peat very slowly how early that morning by some camellias he'd found a girl like a little kitten whose name was going to be Cecília.

Geneva, October 1963—December 1965

MERCÈ RODOREDA WAS BORN IN BARCELONA IN 1909, at a time when Catalonia was autonomous and its citizens were allowed to speak, write, and study their own language. She published five novels between 1932 and 1937, and then fled to Paris and then Geneva from the brutal suppression of Catalan culture. She did not publish again until 1959, when her novels and short stories became a fixture on Catalan best-seller lists. When Franco died, Rodoreda returned to Barcelona, where she stayed until she died of cancer in 1983.

DAVID H. ROSENTHAL'S 1983 TRANSLATION OF THE 15th-century Catalan novel *Tirant lo Blanc* was the first English publication of that work. He also translated several contemporary Catalan authors, including Rodoreda's *The Time of the Doves* and *My Christina*. Rosenthal is also the author of several volumes of poetry, books about jazz, and a book about Barcelona called *Flags in the Wind*. He earned his doctorate in comparative literature from the City University of New York, and taught at colleges in New York and Spain. Rosenthal died of cancer in 1992.

C O L O P H O N

This book was designed by Jean Foos and Dirk Rowntree.
It is set in Fairfield type by The Typeworks and manufac-
tured by Edwards Brothers on acid-free paper.